CAPSIZED

Acclaim for Julie Cannon's Fiction

In *Smoke and Fire*... "Cannon skillfully draws out the honest emotion and growing chemistry between her heroines, a slow burn that feels like constant foreplay leading to a spectacular climax. Though Brady is almost too good to be true, she's the perfect match for Nicole. Every scene they share leaps off the page, making this a sweet, hot, memorable read."—*Publishers Weekly*

Breaker's Passion is... "an exceptionally hot romance in an exceptionally romantic setting. ...Cannon has become known for her well-drawn characters and well-written love scenes." —*Just About Write*

In *Power Play*... "Cannon gives her readers a high stakes game full of passion, humor, and incredible sex."—*Just About Write*

About *Heartland*... "There's nothing coy about the passion of these unalike dykes—it ignites at first encounter and never abates. ...Cannon's well-constructed novel conveys more complexity of character and less overwrought melodrama than most stories in the crowded genre of lesbian-love-against-all-odds—a definite plus."—Richard Labonte, *Book Marks*

"Cannon has given her readers a novel rich in plot and rich in character development. Her vivid scenes touch our imaginations as her hot sex scenes touch us in many other areas. *Uncharted Passage* is a great read."—*Just About Write*

Visit us at www.boldstrokesbooks.com

By the Author

Come and Get Me

Heart 2 Heart

Heartland

Uncharted Passage

Just Business

Power Play

Descent

Breakers Passion

Rescue Me

I Remember

Smoke and Fire

Because of You

Countdown

Capsized

CAPSIZED

by

Julie Cannon

2016

CAPSIZED

ISBN 13: 978-1-62639-479-7

This Trade Paperback Original Is Published By
Bold Strokes Books, Inc.
P.O. Box 249
Valley Falls, NY 12185

First Edition: April 2016

CREDITS
EDITOR: SHELLEY THRASHER
PRODUCTION DESIGN: SUSAN RAMUNDO
COVER DESIGN BY SHERI (GRAPHICARTIST2020@HOTMAIL.COM)

Acknowledgments

With this, my fourteenth book, I continue to be amazed that I am doing this and I have the support of so many people to make it possible. Obviously, my number one thanks to my publisher, Len Barot, for making it all happen for all the writers and readers of Bold Strokes Books. My editor extraordinaire, Shelley Thrasher, who keeps me honest and teaches me something with every manuscript. All the people behind the scenes that make our stories come alive and our dreams come true.

Dedication

For my family and all the fun times we have on our boat.

PROLOGUE

You're under arrest for..."
I didn't hear the rest of the conversation, the pain and humiliation drowning out the words I thought I would never hear in my life. The snap of the handcuffs was louder than I expected. The muscles in my shoulders tensed and my head started to pound. This couldn't be happening, not to me. I was always so careful, never letting my emotions override my logic.

When did it start to go wrong? When did I begin to lose control? When had my life gone from carefully choreographed to a bad B movie complete with two guys who looked exactly like Munch and Stabler in *Law and Order SVU* and prison gray? Or was it prison orange now?

The woman across the room glared at me, her eyes filled with hate. I wanted to turn away, my shame almost too much to bear, but I forced myself to look at her, the woman I'd given my heart, and so much more to. The one woman I'd let in. The woman whom I daydreamed about and was building a life with. Or I was until these two men came knocking on my door three weeks ago.

Now all I saw was the bitch who had connived her way into my heart and would forever be the source of my worst nightmare. My girlfriend, partner—my God, I was even thinking about proposing to her! My knees almost buckled at what that betrayal could have cost me. But right now, as the two FBI agents escorted

Ariel Sinclair out of my office in handcuffs, I couldn't think about anything but what I needed to do to make sure no one ever made a fool of me again.

My hands shook as I closed my office door. By sheer force of will I calmly crossed the room and sat behind my desk. The leather chair conformed to my rigid spine as I leaned back and stared at the items in front of me.

Next to the requisite stapler, telephone, and in-box sat the framed picture of me and Ariel in Beijing—the only personal photo in my large office. I had gone to the famous city six months ago to negotiate a contract with a local manufacturer of cereal that would propel my company far above my closest competitor. The deal was critical to my long-term-growth strategy, and I was so optimistic I would get it I'd taken Ariel along.

I stared at the picture. We were standing together, our arms around each other as the sun set over the mountains, the Great Wall stretching out behind us. We had hurried back to the hotel, our desire for each other exploding the instant the hotel room door closed behind us. We'd made love fast, feeding off each other, straining for connection, driving for release.

I studied the photo, dissecting every inch of Ariel as I searched for what I'd missed. So this was what a corporate spy looked like, at least the one that had infiltrated my company. Did her smile really illuminate her eyes? Was the arm wrapped around my shoulders forced? Was she really holding me, or was I just a prop in her game? Did Ariel feel anything for me? Was every word scripted, every touch a part of the job description of an industrial spy? Did she get paid according to the number of orgasms she gave me, or was that just part of her sick way of dominating me?

"God damn it!" I shouted and hurled the picture across the room. It hit the wall, the glass breaking into pieces. Those were the first words I'd uttered since the two FBI agents had entered my office ten minutes ago. Ariel had said plenty, professing her innocence to deaf ears. I had seen the evidence, most of which

I hadn't provided, and it was overwhelming. What the Munch clone had told me shocked me. How had Ariel obtained so much information? Obviously being the boss's girlfriend opened a lot of doors, computer files, and mouths.

Agitated, I paced back and forth in front of the large window. The lights of the city sparkled in the dark night, and the sight always reminded me of the stars in the clear sky when I was on my boat. Tonight they mocked me almost as if every one of them were a sign of Ariel's betrayal I'd missed due to my stupidly falling under the spell of a beautiful, charming woman.

"Never again," I said as if standing in front of my maker. "Never again will I let my heart or my body rule my brain. It will never happen again." I emphasized every word.

Feeling the first brick of my resolve start to rebuild, I squared my shoulders and threw the broken frame and photo into the trash can under my desk. The move was functional and symbolic at the same time. Ariel was trash, what we'd had together tossed out with the day's garbage.

Even though no one could see me, I held my head high as I walked across the plush carpet on the floor, past the plaques on the wall and statues on the tables that all symbolized my success. My professional life remained intact, although a bit tattered, but only I and a few other people knew what had happened. My personal life, however, was in shambles, splintered into a thousand pieces by one conniving bitch. Everyone would continue to see the first, and no one would ever see the second.

I closed my office door behind me. My new life began tomorrow at eight a.m.

CHAPTER ONE

Alissa

I gripped the wheel tight, the polished silver slick and almost slipping through my wet hands. The wind whipped the few strands of my hair that always refused to be secured in my ponytail, irritating the hell out of me. The slip was smaller than I was used to, and the people on the dock watching me pull in didn't bother me in the least.

When I went to buy my boat, the first salesman I encountered had told me in a somewhat condescending tone that the boat I was looking for, the Catalina 357, was too big for one person to sail alone. I knew he really meant that a woman couldn't control a sophisticated craft like the 357.

I'd caught him checking me out more than once as he showed me around the gleaming showroom asking questions to determine if I was a serious buyer, had a sugar daddy, or was just a lookie-loo. He didn't need to know if I planned to finance or pay cash; he just needed to tell me what I wanted to know about the boat.

He copped a serious attitude when I told him as much, and I walked out and bought a bigger model, the Catalina 387, from a dealer a few miles away. I couldn't help but grin when I returned to the original dealer later that day and told the manager as much. I winked at the salesman as I walked out, reminding him of the steep commission he'd lost due to his stupid, chauvinistic attitude.

I'd been sailing my boat single-handedly after that for years. Occasionally I'd had company—friends and family and on those rare occasions when I'd met somebody who not only held my interest for more than a night or two but knew what they were doing on the water as well.

My mother exposed me to the love of water when I was old enough to fit safely into a life vest. She'd been on the U.S. Olympic team competing in the double sculls and eights, where she and her teammates captured two gold medals in women's rowing. She still met with her fellow crew members at least once a year, and one time I'd been invited to go along. Listening to those women, now in their late fifties, talk about what they had accomplished well before I was born was inspiring. Now, one was an aeronautical engineer for NASA, two were attorneys, one a physician, one CEO of a software company that just went public, one a foster mother of no less than seventeen children, one a Peace Corps volunteer, and, of course, my mother. As a child instead of asking for a bedtime story I'd ask my mom to tell me about rowing in the Olympics and the medal ceremony. When other little girls were pretending to be moms and teachers, I practiced my wave on the gold-medal stand.

My dad taught me the importance of hard work, dedication, and wanting something bad enough to sacrifice for it. He also taught me how to sail, and his words were echoing in my head as I pulled into the slip. *Keep the vessel in the middle of the channel. Keep your movements slow and even. It's just like parking a car. Watch your angles, your speed, the dock on either side. Don't look at the people around you. Pull right into the center of the slip, then angle to the side where you're going to dock. Slowly use the engines to maneuver, slowly, slowly, and stop. Perfect.*

The harbormaster had assigned me to slip fourteen on the other side of Boston Harbor from the one I paid a small fortune for. An adjacent slip was undergoing construction, and I'd requested and been given a different one until work was completed. No need to tempt fate that a stray nail, piece of plywood, or slab of concrete would find its way aboard my boat. The crisp late-April air signaled that spring was on the way.

My parents had sent me to the best schools in an attempt to instill more discipline and rigor in me, but it didn't work. I was creative, not one to follow the rules or stay between the lines, as the saying goes. My mind had a hard time shutting down, the creative juices spilling out and over the cup. More often than not I was in trouble, taking my friends along with me until they wised up and realized the thrill wasn't worth the punishment. My dad had a favorite saying: "You can choose your actions, but you can't choose the consequences." I never *suffered* the consequences, because to me the experience was worth it.

Two days after I graduated with a master's degree in advertising from the University of Florida, I moved to Boston and started work at Bloom and Gross. B&G, as the firm was known, was one of the premier ad agencies in the Northeast. Our client list contained many household names, and I thought I'd died and gone to heaven—another of my father's sayings.

I was twenty-one years old, young, pretty, and talented. At least that's what everyone at B&G told me. Well, not the young-and-pretty part; those just helped me get laid. During the eight years I was there I was given challenging assignments, made a name for myself, and took home a load of money. I was working eighty hours a week and had no time to spend it, so when I left B&G to start my own firm, I had money in the bank and a reputation that followed me.

Alissa Cooper Advertising. Okay, so it's not the most clever agency name, but why mess with a sure thing? Alissa Cooper was in the black in only two years. After eight years and fourteen employees, eight of them new as a result of the Ariel fallout, I had gross revenue of 2.6 million dollars. That's when I bought the 387, christened it *Adventures*, and spent as much of my precious free time on the water as I could.

Now, after securing the bow and stern to the dock, I locked the main cabin and headed to the office.

"Miss Cooper." The tall, thin old man behind the counter greeted me. "Get her tucked in?" He was referring to the docking of my boat.

"Yes, Robert, I did." I glanced around. The harbor office hadn't changed in forever, though boxes of gum and tubes of sunscreen and ChapStick had replaced the rain parkas folded into a four- by five-inch pouch that had sat on the counter during my last visit. Robert reached behind him and grabbed a manila folder with my name stenciled in bold black letters on the tab.

We exchanged small talk as I filled out the paperwork. I didn't bother reading the fine print. Because I'd requested a temporary accommodation for *Adventures*, I handed over my American Express card, initialed the bottom of pages one and two, and scrawled my name above the line on page three.

"Can I get you anything else, Miss Cooper?" Robert asked, always one to go the extra mile.

"No, thanks, Robert. I'm headed home. See you tomorrow." I pocketed my copies of the paperwork as the bell on the top of the door rang twice when I pulled it shut behind me.

The late-afternoon sun was warm on my back. I'd been out on the water all day, and the burning on the nape of my neck signaled that I'd forgotten to put sunscreen on again. I'd seen firsthand the damage the sun can do to unprotected skin and had made it a habit to liberally apply SPF 30. But I always forgot that one spot. Maybe it was because it was hidden under my hair, or maybe by the time I reached that part of my body I was bored with the routine and just wanted to get on with launching *Adventures*. Either way, even with a pretty good base tan, I'd be sporting a red neck for a few days.

I passed a few familiar faces as I walked the eight blocks to my house. It had been a beautiful day, and I felt more relaxed than I had in a long time. Any time aboard *Adventures* provided me a calm respite from the craziness of my life, and today was no different. For a nanosecond I'd toyed with the idea of inviting Jackie, the woman I'd been seeing lately, but quickly realized that not only did we have little, if any, sizzle between us, but also she probably wouldn't have the first clue about sailing. I'd spend the day babysitting instead of relaxing. Even with the possibility of some much-needed sex, I didn't want the potential aggravation. God, I had to be getting old if the idea of an orgasm came in second to the irritation I might have to endure to get it.

I shook my head and chuckled as I rounded the corner of my block. My house was the third one from the corner and the forest-green door my welcome mat. All the houses on the block had the same floor plan, with steps leading up to the front door, bay windows on the first and second floors, and a flat front on the third one. Our block stood out because every owner had painted their exterior a bold, bright color. The Stevenses' place on the corner was blue, the gay guys' house next to me a wonderful shade of gray, and mine was an eye-popping red. The colors continued down the street, and all of us had painted our trim a blistering white.

I'd bought my place for the location and potential—two of the major things I was looking for. I'd renovated it from top to bottom, and next to *Adventures*, it was my sanctuary from the stress of daily life. When the weather prevented me from sailing I'd often close the door behind me on a Friday evening and not open it again until seven a.m. Monday morning.

I glanced at my watch as I slid my key into the lock. Just enough time to toss something on the grill, enjoy a glass or two of wine, and prepare for another crazy week at Alissa Cooper Advertising. But I was Alissa Cooper, and I absolutely loved my job.

CHAPTER TWO

Bert

I couldn't stop looking at the woman to my right as she too was obviously picking up a few things in the market. I did a double-take because she looked like Charlize Theron. She was maybe an inch or two shorter than my own five foot nine inches, with more than a few gray strands scattered in her long blond hair. Women who wore their age and experience proudly were just plain sexy. And this woman was. She hadn't said or done anything, but she oozed sensuality. She obviously had stopped by the market on her way home from work because she was wearing a perfectly tailored expensive business suit and shoes that made her legs look very long.

But what the hell did I know? I'm a fisherman, and my wardrobe consists of jeans, skid-resistant boots, and a flannel shirt, all under a bright-orange head-to-toe slicker. What I did recognize was a silver Breitling watch circled her left wrist. I'm a bit of a watch snob, and for some reason the large, expensive, yet practical watch was one of the sexiest things I'd ever seen. Jeez, if an expensive watch on a beautiful woman's wrist was all it took to get my motor running, I really needed to get out more.

The cashier pulled me out of my fantasy when she told me my total. I reached for my credit card in my back pocket, and a jolt of panic shot through me when my hand didn't feel the familiar stiff card. Shit, where was it? Just as quickly I remembered that I'd last used it at the harbor gas pumps and had probably left it there. I quickly searched my other pockets and came up with a few crumpled worn bills. I was four dollars and eighty-two cents short.

"Shit, I left my card at the harbor office," I said, completely embarrassed. "Can you hold this? I'll be back in ten minutes to pay for it." Before the cashier had a chance to answer, the woman I'd been ogling spoke.

"I'll get it."

Her voice was smooth and a tingle ran down my spine. Her eyes were crystal blue, the color of the Caribbean. A small bump on her nose was the only imperfection on her smooth, tan face.

"Thank you, but you don't have to do that. I'll just come back," I said politely. Even though I owned a commercial fishing boat, employed a crew of six men, and spent ninety percent of my time with them fishing the waters off the coast, my mother had raised me with manners. And more importantly, I still used them, especially in front of a beautiful woman. The woman smiled and my mouth went suddenly very dry.

"Consider it my public service for the day." She pulled a five-dollar bill out of her wallet and handed it to the cashier.

"Thank you," I managed to reply and was rewarded with another dazzling smile. The woman gathered her bags and started to leave, but I couldn't let her get away.

"Can I buy you a cup of coffee to thank you?" God, did that ever sound like a pick-up line. But then again I was a little out of practice. No, I was a lot out of practice. The woman laughed, and I thought I'd melt right there on the floor in the front of her.

"You don't have any money." She grinned at me this time.

"We can go to the Port Café. We have to pass right by where I left my card when I paid for my gas." I hoped I didn't sound as desperate as I felt, or as lame.

The woman's eyebrows quirked, which I thought was really cute. "No, really," I said quickly. "I just docked and paid for my gas and came in to pick up a few things." My explanation sounded stupid, but it was the truth.

I could almost hear her weigh her choices, which probably consisted of having a drink with me or enjoying dinner with a beautiful, sophisticated woman, not one in faded jeans and a Henley. The only thing I had going for me at this instant was that my shirt brought out the green in my eyes, or so I'd been told.

"It's just coffee," I said, filling the awkward silence. Then I said something really stupid. "I'm not asking you to have a baby with me." Fortunately she must like stupid because she laughed.

"All right," she said, and I had to fight to not let my mouth drop open. I have a lot of confidence, but even I thought this woman was a long shot.

I extended my hand. "Bert Coughlin."

She took it, her handshake firm and electric. "Alissa Cooper."

Chapter Three

Alissa

I watched Bert's reaction to my acceptance. Bert? What an odd name. I'd have to ask about that later. It hadn't taken me long to answer her invitation. My choices for tonight consisted of going home to my empty house and spending the evening working on the papers I'd jammed in my briefcase or sitting across from a woman who, for some odd reason, I found interesting. It had been too long since I just relaxed and enjoyed myself. I'd had an absolutely shitty day, and the thought of another night of numbers and reports suddenly didn't appeal to me very much.

After Ariel, I didn't trust any woman, but it wasn't like Bert and I would talk about profit-and-loss statements, my current projects, or my client list. Like I'd discuss that with anyone ever again. And when Bert had unequivocally stated "It's just coffee. I'm not asking you to have a baby with me," that clinched it. I liked her sense of humor, or what I'd seen of it so far, and she was nothing like any woman I'd ever met. And I mean NOTHING. I don't consider myself a social snob, but most people hang out with the people they work with or play with. The former, I didn't do. I had difficulty maintaining boss-employee distance, especially when it came to discipline, so I tried not to tempt fate. The latter took me to the gym, the symphony, dinner with a few close friends, and my boat. Bert was nowhere in that picture.

Her hands were rough and callused, and she had more than a few lines around her eyes. Neither was unattractive, and suddenly I was very curious about the origin of both. She was a little taller than I was, her jeans looked as comfortable as my favorite pair, and the color of her shirt reflected her brilliant green eyes.

Don't think like that, I told myself. This is coffee, nothing else, and certainly not a hookup. It had been a long time since I'd gotten any, other than what I gave myself, but this was not going there. I wasn't in the mood and knew I wouldn't get in the mood either after the day I'd had. Some of my friends can go home after a lousy day and leave their office drama at their front door. Sherrie had a knockout husband who couldn't keep his hands off her, Joanne and Stephanie had two kids, and Michelle had just had a baby. No sex for her for the next six weeks, per doctors' orders. I've often thought that way back in history some exhausted woman had begged her doctor to tell her husband that just so she could get some sleep. Both Michelle and my sisters concurred with my hypothesis.

I stowed my few groceries in the trunk of my car, and Bert and I walked to the office where you paid for gas. She hadn't lied, using the "I forgot my wallet can I go get it and buy you a drink" line, which was a relief. The cashier greeted her by name and handed her the AWOL card before she had a chance to ask. The harbor hadn't yet adopted the pay-at-the-pump, and everyone from the smallest personal craft to the largest fishing boat had to go inside and pay. It was a great marketing strategy to get people into the store.

We had a short walk to the Port Café and made small talk, not getting into anything heavy or controversial, which was refreshing. Against my better judgment I found myself wanting to know more about Bert—what she did for a living, how often she was on the water, what her lips tasted like. Holy shit, where had that come from? I'd just met the woman and I was thinking about that? I really needed to get out more—or stay in more, and definitely not alone.

The cafe was a quaint restaurant that had been here on the dock forever, or so the locals said. I'd been inside once or twice, but my local haunt was the Harbor Club, as upscale as its name implied. "The Club," as it was known, was open only to members of the yacht club, where everyone was greeted by name when they entered. It had over four hundred members and associate members, and in the beginning I was impressed and then realized that, with the hefty membership fee and annual dues, they should know everyone by name.

The bell over the door dinged when Bert pulled it open. The smell of something delicious on the barbecue and fresh-baked pie greeted me when I stepped inside. The place was decorated in a nautical theme, as it should be right next to the water, but had charm that made it feel authentic, something you'd find inside one of the small bungalows a few blocks away. I wasn't hungry in the slightest, or at least I wasn't until a waitress carrying a plate of delicious-looking shrimp passed in front of me. I didn't know exactly what time it was, but I'd left work a little after four thirty, then had a thirty-minute commute, the stop at the market, and the walk to pick up Bert's credit card, so it had to have been around six. If coffee went well, maybe we could have dinner. But only because my mouth was watering from the delicious smells coming from the kitchen. I mean a girl's gotta eat, right?

❖

Bert

As we strode to the café I caught the scent of Alissa's perfume. It was fresh, not heavy, and it smelled expensive. Like I know what expensive smells like. I bought my shampoo and lotion at Walgreens, maybe Target if I needed a bunch of other things. I had to walk quickly to keep up with her, I guess an offshoot of whatever she did that necessitated her power suit and her quick, no-nonsense stride. She kept her head up, didn't slouch or stoop to try to be something she wasn't. That kind of confidence was just flat-out sexy. It said I know who I am and what I am, and I'm not afraid of it. If you are, your loss. I opened the door and Alissa stepped inside.

"Bert, we haven't seen you in ages," Clarisse said a second after we entered. The only way I can adequately describe Clarisse is to say she was buxom, had big hair—and I mean BIG hair—and she could have been Anna Nicole Smith's twin sister. Her smile filled her face and her laugh was contagious. She rarely met a customer she didn't like. I'd known Clarisse all my life. This was her place, and the café was a staple of Colton Harbor. When I used to come in with my dad she was larger than life, and the first few times I was afraid of her. Of course I was four or five years old at the time, and a woman who occupied as much space as Clarisse, with her boobs, hair, and gregarious personality, would scare any little kid.

"Good to see you too, Clarisse. How's life?"

"Making money and making friends," she answered. If I had a dollar for every time I heard that phrase, my boat would be paid for. If only. I caught Clarisse checking out Alissa, then looking to me with a question in her eyes before she winked at me.

"We're just going to have a something to drink," I said, informing Clarisse this was just a friendly chat, not the prelude to something more.

She grabbed the menus and stated, "I'll put you in the back. It's a little quieter there."

I motioned for Alissa to go ahead, again out of politeness, but it also gave me the opportunity to check out her backside. I'd figured out a long time ago why men always let women go first. It had probably started hundreds of years ago so they could check out the ladies' asses without getting their faces slapped. More than likely it started in England, where the definition of gentleman was invented. It was rude to blatantly ogle women, but if you held the door and let them go first, not only did you get to be close to them, but you could smell their perfume or shampoo as they walked by, with the added benefit of having an unobstructed view of their ass. Thank God for gentlemen and manners, I thought as I followed Alissa to our table.

Clarisse kept up a running conversation with Alissa, who seemed to be oblivious to the men watching her cross the room and the not-so-gentlemen turning their heads for an additional look when she passed them. I couldn't blame them and enjoyed the view.

Clarisse set menus on the table in front of us and said, "Just in case something to drink turns into dinner." She winked at me and I felt myself blush. "I'll send Marcus right over." And with that, she turned and walked away.

"She's quite the character," Alissa commented.

"Yes, she is." And before I could say anything more, Marcus arrived.

"Ladies, how are you this evening?" He turned to Alissa. "My name is Marcus and I'll be taking care of you tonight." He then turned to me. "Bert, good to see you again. How long has it been? A month, two?" Marcus frowned as he apparently tried to remember the last time I was in. It had been a long time, but the actual length really didn't matter.

"It's been a while, Marcus. How are you?"

"I'm fine. Had a stomach bug last week, but Stephen took good care of me and I'm back on my feet."

"Stephen is Marcus's boyfriend," I told Alissa.

"You've been gone too long, Bert. You missed the big announcement. We're engaged. He's the one." He had a dreamy look in his eyes as he raised and lowered his dark eyebrows a few times.

"My apologies and congratulations, to you and Stephen, Marcus."

"How long have you two been together?" Alissa asked pleasantly, surprising me by asking.

"Fourteen months," Marcus answered proudly.

"Then I second the congratulations. When's the big day?" Again she surprised me.

"We haven't set a date yet, but probably in the fall. Enough about me though. Clarisse will skin me if I don't stop chattering and take your order," he said, pen and pad in hand like a messenger ready to carry an important dispatch behind enemy lines.

"I'll have decaf," Alissa said.

"Leaded for me, Marcus. Thanks."

"Anything to snack on? The calamari is fresh and out of this world," he said with a flair.

I looked at Alissa, my expression saying "up to you." She declined, and I sent Marcus on his way to get our coffees.

"Obviously you come here often," Alissa observed, leaning back in the booth.

"What was your first clue?" I discovered that I liked to tease her. "Actually I live not far from here." I remained vague, not wanting to give this strange yet beautiful woman anything more specific. I'd made that mistake once and it wasn't pretty. Can you say Shawna stalker? "I don't cook much. It's easier to come in here, friendlier too." I lived alone, and as much as I liked myself, my company got a little boring sometimes. And lonely. "What about you?"

"Same," she answered as Marcus set two cups of steaming hot coffee down in front of us, then discreetly disappeared. She reached for the sugar bowl and poured four heaping spoons into her cup. Holy cow. My lips puckered at all that sweetness. Alissa must have noticed my expression.

"I never learned to like black coffee," she said, her spoon tinking against the side of the mug. "I had to drink it in college to stay awake and just kept adding sugar until I could stand it. Not the healthiest thing in my diet, I admit. Too many years to try to reprogram my taste buds, and too old to try."

I liked Alissa. She had a good sense of humor and didn't seem to mind poking fun at herself. And she'd talked to Marcus. Too many people ignored their server, and that was just rude. That and Marcus was a friend of mine.

"I guess I could say the same. Too many years of drinking sludge to stop now. My body would probably rebel from the sheer shock without it."

"What do you do that sludge is a mainstay of your daily intake?"

Here it was. The inevitable "what do you do" question. Why didn't get-to-know-you questions start off with topics like the latest political race or the state of the economy or the losing streak of the Toronto Blue Jays? I had an instant to decide to tell the truth or make something up. Oddly enough I took the former.

"I'm a fisherman."

Alissa looked puzzled. "A fisherman? Like a charter boat or commercial?"

That was the third time Alissa had surprised me. No one ever even thought of commercial fishing. "Commercial."

"Really? I know nothing about commercial fishing. Tell me about it. How big is your boat, what do you fish for?"

"I have a one hundred, fifty-three-foot schooner with twin Cat 353 engines rated at eight hundred and fifty total horsepower with thirty-eight thousand gallons of fuel capacity and ten thousand gallons of water. I carry a crew of six." Usually at this point eyes glazed over.

"Wow," Alissa said, her expression copying the awe in her voice. "I beg your pardon, Captain. You have a ship, not a boat."

A tingle spun around in my stomach. I liked the way she called me Captain and returned her playful salute. "Well, you know…size matters," I said, tipping my head to say "you know what I mean." Where in the hell had that come from? Sure, this woman was beautiful, charming, and had loaned me four dollars and eighty-two cents, but I hadn't had any intention of flirting with her. Just a polite thank you.

"Spoken by someone who has something big enough to brag about? But I prefer finesse rather than brute strength most of the time," she added, her tone sultry.

I choked on my coffee and was thankful it didn't come out of my nose. That would have been more than a little humiliating. After wiping my mouth I looked at Alissa. Her eyes were twinkling, yes, twinkling with mischief. Interesting. Very interesting. I let my eyes wander over her face, and when they landed back on hers I detected more than playfulness in them now. The tingling in my stomach dropped farther south.

"What do you fish for?" Alissa asked.

It took me a few moments to realize she'd changed the subject. Dang, it was just getting good. "Bluefin tuna."

"Like *Tuna Wars*?" Alissa asked referencing the popular, if not more than a little melodramatic reality show.

"No, not nearly so dramatic." I was starting to really like Alissa. She was inquisitive and appeared to be genuinely interested.

"I can honestly say I've never met a fisherman before, especially one with a one hundred fifty-three-foot schooner with twin Cat 353 engines rated at eight hundred fifty-three total horsepower, with thirty-eight thousand gallons of fuel capacity and ten thousand gallons of water."

It was my turn to be surprised. She'd been paying attention.

"Why don't you call yourself a fisherwoman?"

I couldn't help but laugh at her question, which she asked with such sincerity. "Because fisherwoman sounds stupid."

She nodded her agreement.

"I'm not the most politically correct person. Sometimes terms like that are just ridiculous."

Marcus refilled our cups. "Everything all right here, ladies?"

Again I deferred to Alissa. I'd invited her and it was her decision.

"Yes, thank you, Marcus."

Damn. I didn't know I'd be disappointed that she hadn't suggested continuing our discussion over dinner until she didn't.

"What about you? And don't tell me you're a bookie. However, if you are, you're a successful one. That suit is very nice," I added, then felt stupid. *That suit is nice.* What a cornball thing to say. Alissa didn't seem to think so.

"Thank you. I'm in advertising."

"In advertising as in radio or television? Or glossy women's magazines filled with stories about how to make the perfect meal and then satisfy your man?" I cringed inside. What in the fuck was I thinking? What in the fuck was I saying? My brain and my mouth seemed to be on two different planets, and I'd crash-landed on the wrong one.

"What makes you think it's not a magazine filled with stories about building the perfect outdoor patio and satisfying your woman?"

Holy Christ, she wasn't at all offended by my stupid comment and threw one right back at me. "Touché," I replied. "I bet you could do both."

Alissa looked at me, her eyes moving over my face, down my neck, and as far down the rest of my body as she could see, the table blocking the really good parts. My throat was suddenly dry and my pulse started to race. She gave me a knowing look. "Actually, I can. And very well, I might add."

Holy double Christ. I had no idea what to say to that. Even if I had intentions of getting this woman into bed, I don't know if I could have said anything. Drool, yes. Say anything substantial, no. I felt like a teenager.

❖

Alissa

I watched Bert decipher the intent behind my words. She had an interesting, open face. Her laugh lines added character, and every one of them probably represented an interesting story

I suddenly wanted to hear. She didn't mask her emotions whether they were curiosity, animation, or interest. And when I say interest, I mean interest in me.

This could be something, could be just what I needed—a simple, uncomplicated fling. But something told me I wouldn't be able to ease into dating Captain Bert. I didn't think Bert did anything less than full throttle. And that possibility was somewhat thrilling.

"At the risk of prying and ruining a perfectly good cup of coffee, I don't think your parents named you Bert."

She spent a few seconds processing the fact that my remark was a question.

"No, they didn't."

"Are you going to tell me what they did name you?" I had my ideas, but I really liked hearing Bert's voice. She talked quickly, but not so fast that her pace was distracting. She had a slight Northeastern accent but again not too much.

"I haven't used it in so long I've forgotten what it is."

"I doubt that," I said. "I'll bet your mother doesn't call you Bert." A flash of what I thought was pain crossed her face, then disappeared. Shit. I'd hit a nerve. I know better than to make a comment like that.

"No, she doesn't." That was all Bert said. There was probably more to her story, but this wasn't the time to dig. "Guess," Bert said, the animation returning to her face.

I was thrilled, to say the least, that I could pull my big fat foot out of my mouth. I looked at her closely. Her hair was short and, with the exception of some salt peppered through it, very dark. Her eyes were green, which I didn't know could happen. But then again I didn't pay that much attention in science class when we studied the section on genetics. I was too busy wanting to discover what was inside Melissa Gary's tight blouse.

"Bertha."

"Bertha?" Bert answered, the smile returning to her face. She was really cute when she smiled. Her face lit up and her eyes sparkled. I'd have to make her do that more often. My pulse kicked up a beat or three.

"No? How about Alberguita?"

"Alberguita? Wasn't that the little girl in *The Sound of Music*?"

"No, that was Brigitta."

"Well?" I asked for confirmation of my guess, knowing full well that wasn't it.

"I'll give you credit for creativity."

"Well, I am in advertising, you know. How about Engelbert? Herbert? Norbert? Robert?" Bert shook her head at each attempt and finally laughed because I was running out of names. Her laugh was deep and uninhibited, and it lit up her entire face. I found myself wanting to hear her laugh for the rest of my life. Whoa, stop right there.

"You have got to be very successful in advertising. You're a nut. If I tell you, will you promise not to laugh?"

I crossed my heart and said as much. Bert's eyes followed my hand, and when she gazed at me, laughter wasn't what I saw in her eyes. Desire was a look I was familiar with, but it was different with every woman. But I couldn't mistake the look. No indeed. My heart beat faster, and a flush of heat coursed through me. Oh dear. This had turned into much more than coffee. Somehow I managed to say, "Only if it's not funny."

She went out on a limb and said, "Alberta Rose Coughlin."

"Alberta Rose Coughlin," I repeated, liking the way the name sounded. "I like it."

"But don't ever call me that. When my mother called me by my full name, I knew I was in trouble. BIG trouble." This time Bert didn't show any sign of pain when she talked about her mother.

"I'll remember that," I said, also noting for future reference that she referred to her mother in the past tense. I wanted to ask if I'd be getting a chance to call her Bert more often, but Clarisse stopped at our table.

"You two going to drink coffee all night or have something to eat?"

I looked at my watch, surprised we'd been talking for over an hour. What I thought would be a perfunctory cup of coffee, minimal, awkward small talk, and then out the door had turned into something else. Something else that was very enjoyable and that, I admitted to myself, I wanted to do again. I started to say as much, but Bert frowned when a scrawny man in a pair of very old overalls quickly approached the table.

"Sorry to interrupt, Captain, but you're needed back on the boat. There's feds on board asking questions," he added with a clear sense of urgency.

Bert turned to look at me, a question in her eyes. It was obvious she needed to go but didn't want to be rude and just leave. I solved the dilemma for her. There was no way, I repeat, no way I was going to have anything to do with anyone who had, what did he call it, "feds on board asking questions." I'd had enough to do with women that law enforcement was interested in.

"Go, I understand," I said, and boy, did I.

Bert said her apologies, tossed a few bills on the table, and hurried out the door behind the little man. She took all the energy out of the restaurant with her.

CHAPTER FOUR

Alissa

Why am I so disappointed? So I lent her a few bucks and shared some laughs over a cup of decaf. That's all I intended it to be so, why do I feel as empty as the seat across from me?

I guess, if I admit it, I liked Bert. She was smart, quick-witted, and funny. She made me laugh, and not many women had been able to do that these last few years. Thank God Olaf, or whatever his name was, came just before I did something stupid like ask her if she had time for dinner.

How did I miss the signs? Probably the same way I missed them with Ariel—a pretty face, sharp mouth, an engaging laugh, and eyes that could suck you right in. But Bert wasn't Ariel, far from it. Whereas Ariel was almost my height and model thin, Bert was several inches taller and solidly built. Ariel was always perfectly coiffed, every hair in place, her makeup perfect; even her lipstick was never smudged. We never made love in the morning until she'd spent at least twenty minutes in the bathroom. Bert, on the other hand, was completely natural, her tanned skin the result of hours spent outdoors instead of in a tanning bed. Ariel had long, graceful, delicate fingers. I was always careful not to squeeze them too hard for fear they'd break. Ariel's touch was always feather-light, almost wispy, even when I begged for something harder.

Bert's looked strong, her nails short and clear of polish. Wonder what those hands would feel like on me?

No, no, no. Do not go there, Alissa Warner Cooper, I told myself as I walked back to my car. Bert was trouble, and even though I could use a good, strong orgasm, or ten or forty about now, I needed to stay away from Alberta Rose Coughlin, and tomorrow was going to be a grueling day.

Four weeks earlier, a messenger had delivered a familiar envelope to my office. I had to personally sign for it, and my hands shook as I opened it. I'd received the exact same envelope about this time for the last three years. I reviewed the contents in my head as I slid the letter opener under the flap. The only unknown was the date of Ariel's next parole hearing.

The letter was addressed to me as the president of Alissa Cooper, and since Alissa Cooper was the victim of the crime and I was the president, I received a notification of any parole hearing. We could choose whether we attended and made our case as to why Ariel should remain incarcerated and complete her full ten-year sentence.

I hadn't been to any of the hearings, sending Paul Houser, the attorney for Alissa Cooper, as our representative. This was more appropriate since the company was the victim, not me personally. Or at least that's what I told anyone who needed to know. So far the parole board had agreed that Ariel needed to remain behind lock and key, but one of these years it might not. A lot of people viewed industrial spying as a victimless crime—no big deal as far as other crimes that people committed. After all, there wasn't really a victim, per se, or so most people thought. Thankfully the jury didn't have that opinion, and Ariel was secured in McDowell Penitentiary for Women.

I read the date printed on the form letter. July seventeenth, a little more than a month from now. Thirty days before Ariel was either set free or remained a guest of the state of Massachusetts until the next letter arrived.

I stood and exited my office. Marie, my administrative assistant, looked up from her keyboard. "I'll be in Paul's office," I said, glancing at her. Paul's office was four doors down the hall from mine, and I used the distance as an opportunity to pull myself together.

"Got a minute?" I asked after knocking on his open door.

"Sure thing, what's up?" Paul replied, removing his glasses and setting them on the stack of papers in front of him. Paul was a very attractive forty-eight, having celebrated his birthday last week. His hair was thinning on top, but with his fit body, engaging manner, and soft North Carolina accent he had most women drooling over him. He'd personally handled the entire Ariel nightmare and worked with my personal attorney to protect me and the firm.

I sat in the chair in front of his desk and crossed my legs. I didn't reply, just handed him the letter. He reached across the desk, his expression shifting from attentiveness to concern. One glance at the official letterhead made him scowl. "I'm an attorney and I understand these things, but when did ten years turn into four or five?"

I knew the question was rhetorical, but I voiced my opinion anyway. "When prisons are filled to overcapacity with murderers and rapists and other violent criminals." I emphasized the word violent. "When there's no more room at the inn, they can't turn on the No Vacancy sign and close the front doors."

Paul didn't reply, just frowned and shook his head as he read the letter again, this time making notes in the margin.

"Do you need anything from me?" I asked, hoping the answer was no.

"I assume you won't be there again this year?"

"I knew you were smart when I hired you." I was trying to add some levity to a dark subject for me. Other than Paul and my personal lawyer, no one knew the full extent of the betrayal. All anyone knew was that Ariel was no longer around, and I let them think I was just no longer seeing her.

Paul stared at me. I knew that look and I didn't like it. "No," I said.

"I think you need to go this year." Paul put his hands up almost defensively before I had the chance to say no fucking way. "Just hear me out on this, Alissa."

"No," I said again.

Paul continued as if I hadn't said anything. "Last year six people were there speaking for Ariel. The DA sent the standard form letter honoring the decision of the court and stating that in the best interest of society we don't support the blah, blah, blah. And then there was me. The pompous, stuff-shirted, corporate bigwig lawyer representing the faceless company." He took a breath and I knew he wasn't done; he'd only just got started. "In the past year sixteen thousand, two hundred, eighty-four people entered the Massachusetts penal system, and do you know how many came out?"

I didn't like where this conversation was going. I didn't answer and knew that Paul didn't expect me to.

"One thousand, four hundred, eighty-two. Prison overcrowding is a hot subject, and the parole board is getting pressure, extreme pressure, to release non-violent prisoners. Namely prisoners just like Ariel."

"But she stole over a million dollars from me. I almost lost my reputation, my firm, for God's sake." And my self-respect, I thought but didn't say.

"They need to hear from you."

"No," I said, adamant. Ariel would be there, and I never wanted to see her again. If I was honest with myself, I don't know if I'd cry or try to strangle her.

"You deserve to have Ariel serve her entire sentence." He hesitated, then added, "Just think about it, Alissa. That's all I'm asking."

He might as well have asked me to go to Mars. My answer would still be the same. Absolutely no fucking way. Now here it was the day before Ariel's hearing, and I was too keyed up to get any work done. I needed fresh air and a walk. What I really needed was to rewind the last six years of my life to the day I met Ariel.

I'd been on the ferry from Camden to Mayfair, my daily trek across the Howard River from my office to my apartment. Twice a day, along with several hundred of my closest friends, I commuted from the 'burbs into the city. It was a warm summer evening when Ariel sat down in the seat next to me.

I was reading a focus-group report, the numbers blurring as I turned the pages. I think I was halfway through the report when I caught a whiff of her perfume. I didn't turn my head, but my eyes moved to my left and caught sight of some very nice cleavage. She crossed her bare legs toward me, and, being a healthy lesbian, I couldn't help but look. They were almost as nice as her chest.

"What are you reading?" Ariel asked.

I thought her opening line was pretty brazen. What business was it of hers what I was reading? But it did the job and got my attention. Well, that and a whole lot of skin. We made small talk under the stars, had dinner by candlelight and sex under her skylight. That was the beginning. For the next two years we were practically inseparable. She moved out of her studio apartment and into my place, and we shared coffee, the commute, and our lives.

We had friends over for dinner on the weekends, hosted football on Sundays, and spent rainy days in bed. We binge-watched *The Sopranos* and reruns of *I Love Lucy*. We'd even started to look for a house, one with a backyard big enough for a swing set. We talked all the time, sharing stories about our day and solving problems. Looking back, I guess I did most of the talking. Ariel had a way of drawing things out of me, wanted to know about even the smallest detail. At first I found it endearing that she wanted to learn so much about my business: who my clients were, what the latest pitch was, and what I was doing to outwit my competitors.

Ariel was a buyer for Fulbright, one of the main department stores in the city. Every three or four months she'd go on a three-week buying trip to Europe, Brazil, and the Far East. At least that's what she told me. When the shit hit the fan, I found out otherwise and my humiliation was complete. Not only was she spying for a rival firm, but she was also married and lived in an upscale apartment in San Francisco with a husband and two cocker spaniels. He thought she was working in Paris and came home during those three-week visits. And to top it all off, her name wasn't even Ariel Sinclair. It was Cindy Howard.

If hindsight were twenty-twenty I'd have never answered her first question. Obviously I wasn't gifted with clairvoyance, and, hindsight being what it is, I made a complete fool of myself over big tits, a pretty face, and a fabulous body. The thought of making love to Ariel still made my stomach turn, as did the monthly blood tests I'd had after she left. It would be just my luck that she would leave me with more than a tattered confidence, shattered heart, and battered psyche. But so far so good, and after two years my doctor finally convinced me I was STD-free. Then why did I still feel dirty and used?

I was a successful professional, college-educated woman. I owned my own firm and had a lot of friends. Why hadn't I seen this coming? Why hadn't I fallen over it when it was right under my nose? Because I had my face buried so deep between Ariel's legs as often as I could I couldn't see anything else. And Ariel made sure I stayed there.

Standing in the checkout line of the grocery store, I, like everybody else, would read the headlines and teasers on the covers of the magazines that flanked the cash registers. I puffed out my chest in pride when I read that I made love at least three times a week more than the average woman—or so the tabloids said. But then again I was definitely not the average woman.

I'd always had a healthy sex drive, and having Ariel in my bed complemented that craving nicely. She was so attentive that if we didn't make love every night and three or four times on the weekend, she made sure to compensate for it. I wasn't complaining. Except for that one time when I had a big presentation the next morning and she kept reaching for me all night. I was exhausted and, even with three cups of coffee and a shot of expresso, was still a bit groggy. I didn't get that account, and today I know why. As a matter of fact, only five people in the world know why: Paul, my personal attorney, my BFF Rachel, me, and Ariel.

Correction, those five and the people who were paying her to spy on me. I swore Rachel to secrecy, didn't tell any of my other friends, my sisters, or my parents. All anyone knew was that I'd stopped seeing Ariel and not had a serious or even semi-serious relationship in almost four years. Everyone finally stopping asking and I never told.

Every time I thought about the beginning of the almost-end I can still smell the FBI agent's aftershave. I could swear it was the same Aqua Velva my grandfather wore. I was working on my speech for the Advertising Association national convention when Jeri, my assistant at the time, knocked on my door.

"Alissa?" she asked after opening my door and poking her head inside. "Two FBI agents are here to talk to you."

Her announcement shifted my attention from irritated to curious. "FBI?" Jeri's head bobbed up and down rapidly, her eyes widening. She was young, and this was her first real job, as she called it, so I forgave her for that reaction. What in the world would I have to say that the FBI would be interested in? I slid my keyboard tray under my desk and stood. "Show them in."

They introduced themselves as Special Agents James Standard and Paul Rutherford, and after we all sat down they proceeded to destroy my world. Eighty minutes later they left and I sat stunned by what they'd told me. To make a long, ugly story short, they had evidence that Ariel had been spying on Alissa Cooper and was trading inside information for cash. *Lots* of cash. They'd stumbled onto the information while investigating another, completely unrelated case and had tracked her down to me.

Everything, from the instant Ariel had first sat down beside me on the ferry to our lunch earlier that afternoon, had been a calculated, well-mapped-out plan. Every day she'd sucked me deeper and deeper into her web, and if it weren't for the accidental discovery she probably would have eaten me alive.

But it had happened. I'd lost a boatload of money, several clients, and eight employees, including Jeri, who had been with me since I opened my own doors, but my firm and I had survived. In the beginning it was simply that—survival. Every day I'd dragged myself out of bed, a dark haze hanging over me, dressed in a don't-fuck-with-me suit, and went out and slayed the advertising dragons. Eventually the fog lifted, the days grew brighter, and I was looking forward more than I was looking back. I don't think I endured any more than anyone else who had their heart broken and dreams shattered, but it was enough for me to say never, ever again.

I stopped at the newsstand on the corner and bought the afternoon paper. Even though my world consisted of computer-generated art, graphics, and images, I was one of those old-school types. I loved the feel of paper in my hand. Whether it was a book, magazine, or like this, the *Local Times*, one of my greatest pleasures was sitting in the warm sun reading.

I grabbed a decaf from Dutch Bros and settled into one of the chairs on their patio. I hadn't walked out my irritation, frustration, or aggravation at having to relive the Ariel thing, but I was calm enough to enjoy the warm, late afternoon. If I took my coffee and paper back to my office I'd be interrupted at least a dozen times before I finished either. I enjoyed my solitude and took advantage of the opportunity.

I turned the page, and the headline of an article caught my eye. FLORIDA LOOPHOLE ALLOWS ILLEGAL FISHING HARVEST. We were nowhere near Florida, but I supposed illegal fishing happened anywhere. Was that what the feds were doing at Bert's boat? Was she doing something she shouldn't be doing?

It had been three days since our coffee chat, and admittedly I'd thought about Bert more than once. Okay, more than a dozen times. Every time I told myself to stop thinking about her, I'd think about her more

She was a commercial fisherman. I'd never met anyone who made their living on the water. Well, yes, I had, but I wouldn't consider the deck hands on the ferry or the waiters on the dinner cruises in the same category as Bert. She definitely was not an Alberta Rose. She was certainly a Bert. She was a little more butch than I'd normally go for, but then again I supposed she'd have to be to gain respect in her chosen field. I didn't know much about fishing and even less about commercial fishing, but my instincts told me it was definitely a man's world.

Yet I found something compelling about her, and I couldn't put my finger on it. Was it because she was so different and I had definitely had enough of women in my own world? With a few exceptions they were either cut-throat competitive in everything, including who was on top, or couldn't add without a calculator.

I'd met many interesting women but had never experienced a spark of anything other than lust, and that was exactly what I was looking for. I wasn't in the market or on the market for anything else. A nice dinner, maybe a movie or a play, stimulating conversation, and stimulating other non-cerebral parts of my body. That's all I wanted, all I could handle, and all I could give. Bert had fit most of the aforementioned qualities, but I'd learned the hard way to listen when the hair on the back of my neck stood up and slapped me. And with Bert I was smart enough to see that reaction coming and ducked just in time.

CHAPTER FIVE

Bert

"I don't know anything else," I said for the fourth or sixth time to Customs Agents Davidson, Shipley, Newman, and Hart. Sounded more like a law firm than four agents from the Department of Homeland Security. Davidson, along with his peers, had come aboard the *Dream* wanting to question me about something I'd reported the day before.

Smugglers and poachers were all over the ocean, and my father had taught me to be obliging, have integrity, and to be a law-abiding citizen. Thus my two-hour conversation with these four men in the bridge of the *Dream*.

By the time the agents left, all but two of my crew had gone home. The others either got bored waiting to find out what was going on or had other obligations. More than likely it was the former. My crew consisted of honest, hardworking men, but unlike most deckhands, who were heavy on booze and women and light on responsibility, mine were family men, solid and dependable. Everyone had drama, comedy, and action-adventure in their lives, but my crew left it on the dock when they came to work. I insisted on it. Commercial fishing was a dangerous profession, and I refused to contribute to the statistics that proved how dangerous it was.

I carried a six-man crew, all experienced on the sea. I didn't tolerate bullshit, laziness, drugs, or booze. I paid well and my crew returned season after season. I respected them, and they me. We all had a job to do and we did it well. Occasionally tempers flared, as they would when seven people are cooped up on a boat one hundred and fifty feet long for weeks at a time. But the anger blew out quickly and we'd move on.

Each of my crew had boat names that fit their personality or experience perfectly. Blow was short for Blowhard because he knew everything, and I mean everything. The unfortunate part was that most of the time he was so full of good-natured bullshit you weren't sure if he was stringing you along or telling the truth. He was well over six feet, built like Smokey the Bear, and had the heavy brown beard to match.

Limpet looked exactly like Don Knotts in the 1964 live-action/ animated adventure film about a man named Henry Limpet, who turns into a talking fish and helps the U.S. Navy locate and destroy Nazi submarines. He was no more than five feet five inches tall and weighed one hundred thirty pounds only when his slicker was soaked and his hip waders full of water. But he took orders and knew his job, the two things most important to me.

Hook was a six-foot, six-inch ex-lineman who'd lost the top of his right ear to a wayward hook the first day on board. When he promptly cleaned up his mess and didn't complain, I knew he was a keeper. Rock could have been Sylvester Stallone's twin brother, in his Rocky heydays. Rock didn't say much, but when he did everyone listened because his message was short, to the point, and always right. Flick, my diver, and Lefty, our cook, rounded out my crew. All of these guys had been my crew for the past eight years, and my life literally depended on them.

"Did they catch them?" Limpet asked, blowing his nose. Along with being scrawny, he had a perpetually runny nose.

"Yes. Eight thousand pounds of cocaine," I answered. That was no surprise to me, as low as the cigarette boat had been riding in the water. Cigarette boat was the term used for sleek, fast boats that drug smugglers often used to slip in undetected or actually outrun the federal agency chasing them. I considered them penis boats because why else would you need something so obvious phallic that was so loud that drew everyone's attention? I kept my opinion to myself while on board the *Dream*.

Limpet whistled. "What I could buy with that," he said almost enviously. My crew might talk smack but they didn't use it. That, and sobriety, were my number two and three boat rules. Number one was safety first in everything we do.

"A whole heap of trouble is what you could buy with that," I answered. Limpet was young and sometime half a brick short of a load, but he was a hard worker and did what he was told, though a bit naive.

"Are we ready for next week?" We were headed out on a six-week trip, one of our longest. With the over-fishing, pollution, and poachers, we had to go out farther each season to catch the same amount of fish we'd grown accustomed to. It would take ten days to reach the fishing area, however many it took to net our catch, and at least two weeks to return to shore. Unfortunately we weren't one of those just-caught-today boats. Restaurants' catch of the day usually came from various farms, where the fish were plentiful and raised commercially in tanks or enclosures. The *Dream* supplied the farms.

"Other than the last-minute perishables, we're ready, Captain."

The perishables Limpet referred to were the fresh fruit, eggs, and vegetables that were delivered the day before we set sail. Lefty was our cook, and he planned the menu and placed the order. The galley had a large refrigerator, a three-burner stove, and a decent-sized oven. We usually had a hot breakfast, sandwiches for lunch, and a hot meal for dinner. If we were really good, Lefty would bake brownies or some other delectable dessert the men would gobble up quickly. We rarely had any leftovers.

I sent Limpet on his way, checked to make sure the security guards I hired were around, and locked the door to the bridge. The additional expense cut into my profits, but with the size of my boat, the hundreds of thousands of dollars' worth of equipment, and the livelihood that it provided for me and six others, I couldn't afford to have anything stolen or, worse yet, sabotaged.

Stepping off the *Dream* I turned and looked at her. She had a royal-blue hull, painted just last year, with white trim and her name on the port and starboard sides. Above the main deck was the bridge with its one-hundred-eighty-degree panoramic view. The fourteen windows were made of tempered glass, so the harsh weather in the open sea would have a next-to-impossible chance to crack or shatter it. Above that, thirty-eight feet above the deck, was the crow's nest, our observation point when we were actually looking for the fish. Numerous cables, supporting wires, and radio antenna were attached to the main rigs and at various points across the top deck. The nets hung from the main mast just aft or behind the bridge. The roof of the bridge could support a small helicopter, but of course I didn't have one of those.

I walked to the parking lot, started my car, and headed home. Sometimes I walked; it was only a mile or so, but I had too much stuff for the boat to carry this morning so I fired up my Jeep instead. Home for me was a forty-eight-foot houseboat moored in the last slip on pier twenty-five. The *Dream* was quietly sitting in slip four at pier six.

Colton Harbor was made up of thirty-two piers, each jutting out into the Atlantic Ocean from the main harbor drive. The harbor was really a peninsula with sixteen piers on both sides and the Harbor Club sitting elegantly at the tip. The Club, as locals called it, offered a three-hundred-and-sixty-degree panoramic view for your drinking, dining, or dancing pleasure. The harbor itself was over eight miles long in total, with shopping strategically placed between every five or six piers. Clever thinking on the part of the designer. That way you didn't have to walk too far to get supplies, a trinket, a souvenir, or gas. It was at one of those small markets where I had met Alissa Cooper.

I thought about Alissa as I drove past the market, then the gas station, then the Port Cafe. I have to admit Alissa was quite an attractive woman. She was engaging, had interesting things to say, and gave me her full attention. She'd hesitated to accept my coffee invitation, but my charm and dazzling smile had obviously won her over. At least that's what I told myself. I was a bit out of practice, but she'd accepted anyway and I'd really enjoyed myself.

I'd been about to ask her if she'd like to continue our conversation into dinner when Limpet came. I'd seen her stiffen at the mention of the feds, but I really hadn't had any time to give it any thought. But now, as I unlocked my front door a little after ten, I did.

Flipping the lights on, I tossed my backpack on the couch and carried the bag of groceries to the kitchen. The smiling face of Alissa Cooper flashed in my mind, and I debated whether to call her when we got back from this trip. She hadn't given me her number, but I could probably track her down. I mean, how many Alissa Cooper advertising agencies could there be in town?

I snickered out loud. Yeah, right. A woman like Alissa would remember me six or seven weeks after just one cup of coffee. She would definitely have moved on.

CHAPTER SIX

Alissa

"No fucking way" four weeks ago turned into me sitting in a room I could only describe as cold, stark, and industrial—and those were its redeeming qualities. The drive here took over an hour, and by the time I parked and passed through three layers of security, my already thin patience was practically nonexistent. My footsteps echoed as I followed a guard down the hall. The air smelled of urine, fear, and despair.

At the front of the room facing me sat three oversized men and two equally plump women, crowded between the ends of a too-small, dented, solid-metal table. I didn't know any of these people, or anyone else in the small, stifling room for that matter, but these five strangers controlled the rest of my life. Okay, maybe that's a little dramatic, but it's the way I felt as I endured being in the hard, uncomfortable chair.

It was Monday, and preparing for this meeting had ruined my entire weekend. I don't know if I was angrier at myself for letting it get to me or the fact that I was here in the first place. I'd spent Saturday and Sunday on my boat, trying not to think about exactly what was happening right now. But everyone knows the more you try *not* to think about something, the more you actually *do*. I've always been able to lose myself on the water, all the stress and crap in my life blowing away with the filling of my sails. The fresh air, warm sun and physical requirements needed to handle the boat usually erase everything in my mind. And if I don't pay attention I could find myself caught up in a line, tossed overboard, or worse.

My heart jumped and my hands started to shake when I heard the door behind me open. Paul had prepared me for the hearing, but I was the only one who could prepare me for the moment Ariel entered the room. She had the right to be present at her own hearing. I sat frozen in anticipation of seeing her for the first time in four years.

Ariel was just as ugly as I remembered her. Sure, she had the same tall, slim body, natural blond hair, and light-blue eyes that once turned every head in the room, on the street, and in the office, including mine. But the instant I found out what she'd done to me and my company she went from runway-beautiful to trailer-trash skank.

Scrutinizing her closer I noticed she carried herself differently. Gone was the self-important, confident, I'm-fucking-the-boss swagger, and in its place were stooped shoulders and a lowered chin. Her once-shoulder-length hair was now chopped off in a blunt cut just below her chin. Her skin held the unhealthy pallor of fluorescent lights instead of the tan from our endless hours on the beaches around the world. Her flat, prison-uniform shoes were nothing like the four-inch stilettos she used to wear every day and, if I were really lucky, to bed. Prison had definitely changed this woman from the Ariel Sinclair I knew to the Cindy Howard she really was.

"Ms. Cooper," the oldest man said. "On behalf of the parole board, thank you for coming." The gold embossing on the name plate in front of him spelled out Chairman Rankin. I didn't need his thanks. I needed him to keep Ariel behind bars. I didn't respond. I just wanted to say what I had to say and get out of here.

"Let me introduce you to the rest of the board," he said and proceeded to do just that. I didn't care who these people were, just as long as they did their job in this case and in every other parole hearing. I'd learned far more about our penal system than I ever wanted to know. The saying that ignorance is bliss sometimes is very definitely true.

"For the record," Chairman Rankin said and nodded toward the stenographer sitting in the corner of the small room, her fingers flying over her silent keyboard. "Note that prisoner 784245 is in attendance." He looked at Ariel. "Would you please state your full name?"

"Cindy Raquel Howard."

The sound of her voice for the first time in all these years jolted me like an electric jolt, and the memories flooded back. I swallowed hard and pushed them aside. I had a job to do. Chairman Rankin then turned to me and asked the same question but added, "And your position in this matter?"

I felt Ariel's eyes on me and cleared my throat. I had stood in front of CEOs of some of the largest, best-known companies in the world and had never experienced the bundle of twitching nerves I felt in front of these civil servants.

"My name is Alissa Cooper. I am the president and owner of Alissa Cooper Advertising. Ariel Sinclair—" I stopped myself. Habit was a bitch. "Cindy Howard pleaded guilty to embezzling one million, four hundred eighty-two thousand, one hundred forty-nine dollars from my firm, conspiracy to thwart fair industrial commerce, and industrial spying." Paul had coached me to be specific and use the official terms of the charges of which Ariel was convicted. Stealing money and customers just didn't have the same punch as the words guilty, embezzlement, conspiracy, and spying.

"Miss Cooper," the man next to Chairman Rankin said, looking through the papers in front of him. "This is the fourth hearing in this matter and only the first time you've bothered to attend."

Okay, now I was really paying attention. His words and the tone in which he used them had a definite meaning. One I didn't like. He hadn't asked me a question so I didn't say anything. Paul had coached me on that too. I waited, knowing his next statement or question would be equally snarky.

"Why is that?" he asked

"Cindy Howard was convicted of those crimes against Alissa Cooper Advertising. I felt it more appropriate to send our legal representative to these hearings." I had to use her full name because *Ms*. Howard was too respectful for her. I knew what was coming next.

"So why are you here now?"

"Because it's important that she remain incarcerated and serve the entire sentence the court handed down."

"And why is that?" the man asked, sitting back in his chair and acting like what I had to say was the most unimportant thing he would ever hear in his life. I forced myself to remain calm. This was an emotional issue for me not only because it was my company but because it was personal. To these five people it was simply their job.

"Because Cindy Howard's actions were illegal and premeditated. She knew what she was doing and continued to perpetuate those actions for years, regardless of who suffered the consequences. She admitted to it, was convicted and sentenced."

"You had a personal relationship with Ms. Howard, didn't you?"

The men were looking at me differently, the women carefully curious. I refused to let this situation slide into a chick-on-chick porno fantasy. I knew I shouldn't but I couldn't stop myself.

"No. She used me to get what she wanted," I said emphatically. "She initiated the contact and employed every means at her disposal to get it." Including her body, I thought but didn't say. In my mind not only was Ariel a criminal, but she was a whore as well.

The other board members asked more questions, and I answered them as succinctly as I could, growing more and more frustrated with the entire proceeding. Finally I had the opportunity to comment versus answer ridiculous questions.

"Cindy Howard methodically and systematically connived her way into a trusted position with Alissa Cooper Advertising. This didn't just happen. She planned this for months and continually refined her plan and her actions as the days went by. This was not opportunistic, a crime of passion, or the result of a negligent act. The judge passed her sentence, and because of her actions you should honor it." There, I had said my piece and couldn't add anything that would convince them one way or the other.

Similar to a jury trial, the prosecution went first, presenting their case. Then the defense presented theirs. I hadn't paid any attention to the others in the room that were here to testify. I knew Ariel's attorney but had no interest in knowing who the others were. I did recognize the man in the dark suit as Ariel's husband, from her trial. Every time I thought of him I couldn't help but picture them making love. Was she the same aggressive cat with him as she was with me? Did she whisper the same sweet sounds? Did she beg him to fuck her harder? Faster? Again? I felt her eyes on me often. This entire morning and the whole Ariel/Cindy thing was surreal.

Ariel/Cindy's attorney spoke next. He glanced over the crimes she'd committed and the extent of her actions but spent most of his time extolling her virtues as a model prisoner. She worked in the library and went to church services every Sunday and bible study on Wednesdays. She had committed one minor infraction of the rules the first week she arrived, but other than that her record was clean. God, he made it sound like she was a pillar of the community—the prison community.

I practically bit the end of my tongue off, not voicing my objection to his statements. There wasn't really anything I could object to, but I could have added "bullshit" to the end of every one of his statements. Ariel/Cindy only did what was in her best interest. If she thought bible study would get her brownie points, she'd go. If she thought scrubbing the toilets with her toothbrush would get her out early, she'd do that too.

"Ms. Howard." The deep voice of the chairman broke into my thoughts. "How do you think you've changed since being here at McDowell?"

My pulse picked up in anticipation of what crap would come out of her mouth.

"I did a terrible thing. I was overwhelmed by greed and lust, and I made a mistake. With the help of my father God and his son Jesus Christ, I have become a different woman. I have seen the error of my ways, the wrong in my actions. I have asked God for forgiveness. I have given my heart and soul to God and will follow wherever He leads me."

What a crock of shit, I thought as I listened to Ariel/Cindy. She was a conniving, manipulating bitch, and you can't change those spots. I didn't believe she'd changed any more than I believed in Santa Claus.

Ariel/Cindy answered a few more questions before she was dismissed. I didn't look at her as she walked out, but I knew she was looking at me. The members of the board asked me a few more questions and then dismissed me too. As I left, Ariel/Cindy's attorney and her husband followed. I hurried down the hall, trying not to look like I was getting the hell out of there as fast as I could.

"Ms. Cooper." A voice behind me called. I didn't want to talk to anyone associated with this case unless it was a member of the board telling me Ariel/Cindy's parole had been denied.

"Ms. Cooper." The voice was closer now. Whoever it was must have hustled to catch up with me. "Ms. Cooper, please, may I speak with you?"

Shit, I was such a sucker for the word please. I stopped and turned around. Ariel/Cindy's husband was standing in front of me, slightly out of breath.

"I don't know what to say other than I'm sorry for what Cindy did to you. I didn't know. Honestly, I had no idea what she was up to."

"Why are you apologizing for her, Mr. Howard?" I asked sincerely.

Obviously that wasn't the response he was expecting, and he had no reply.

"If you didn't know, then I'm truly sorry for you because then she fucked us both."

With those parting words of wisdom I turned around and walked out of the building.

CHAPTER SEVEN

Bert

"Captain, Captain!" I woke to Limpet pounding on my door. By the tone of his voice I knew something was wrong. I shot out of bed, grabbed my shorts, and while yanking them on I hopped to the door. Glancing at the clock I saw it read one forty-two. I'd been asleep for only a little more than two hours.

"What is it?" I asked, zipping my pants. I slept in a T-shirt so at least that part of me was already covered. Not that it mattered. My crew had seen me almost naked on more than one occasion over the past eight years. I slid my feet into my boots.

"We picked up a woman in the water."

"What?" Sometimes Limpet didn't always make sense.

"We picked up a women in the water," he said excitedly. "Blow saw a flashing light, and when we got there the woman was in the water. She had on a life vest with an emergency light. She's in the galley."

I struggled to put the pieces together of what he was saying. We were in the middle of nowhere and someone was in the water?

Stepping through the watertight doorway, I immediately saw the woman sitting at the table, one of our blankets draped around her shoulders. Her hair was wet and she was shivering. I smelled fresh coffee and noticed her hands shake as she reached for the mug in front of her. Lefty was sitting across from her, a pen and tablet in his thick, large hands. When he saw me, relief covered his face.

"Captain," he said, practically jumping out of his chair. The woman turned and I stopped, Limpet running into me from behind. I stopped because I was staring into the beautiful blue eyes of Alissa Cooper.

"Alissa?" That was all I could say. She looked around, apparently equally shocked.

"Is this your boat?" she asked after a few seconds.

"Yes, she is. What happened?" I grabbed the chair Lefty eagerly vacated and took a sip of the coffee Limpet brought me.

"My boat was on fire," she said. "I grabbed a life vest and jumped."

Holy crap. We were six days out of port and she was out here? "Was anyone with you?" I asked, hoping the answer was no. It would be next to impossible to find anyone in this water. It had been a miracle that Blow saw her.

"No. I was by myself."

By herself? Out here in the middle of the Atlantic Ocean? "Did you get a mayday out?" I looked at Blow, who shook his head. If she had, we would have picked it up on our scanner.

"No." She tried to say more, but her teeth were chattering so hard she couldn't finish. She shook her head instead.

I noticed her shoulders were bare. Did she even have any clothes on? No way would she be able to warm up with just coffee. "Come with me," I said, taking her by the arm. "You need a hot shower and warm clothes." I turned to Limpet. "We'll notify the coast guard after she gets warm and tells us what happened. I'll get her settled and be up in a minute."

The corridors weren't wide enough for two, so I stepped in front of Alissa and took one hand while she used the other one to hold the blanket around her. Her hand was ice cold and I increased my pace. We entered my cabin, and I went directly to the shower and turned on the water. With every inch at a premium on a boat, I had taken out the conventional water heater and installed a tankless one. Not only did we have hot water almost instantly, but I got an additional eight square feet of shower stall.

I pulled the blanket off Alissa's shoulders and handed her a clean towel. "Get in," I said. "There's only enough water for a six-minute shower, but it's hot." I hadn't bought a desalinization tank yet. It was a luxury I couldn't afford. "I'll get you some dry clothes."

"Thanks," Alissa said, her teeth chattering. She turned and stepped into the shower but not before her naked butt drew my attention. I didn't glance or catch a glimpse or sneak a peek; I looked. Some might call me a pig, their opinion that this wasn't the time or place to check her out, but, hey, I'm a healthy lesbian, and I admit to admiring a beautiful woman regardless of the situation. I didn't stop looking until she closed the opaque shower door behind her.

As I started to leave, Alissa screamed. I yanked open the door. She was as far away from the water as she could get, the palms of her hands covering her breasts.

"What is it? What's the matter?" I looked at her trying to figure out what was wrong.

"The water…" was all she was able to say in between sobs.

"Alissa, what is it? What's the matter?" I asked, sounding stupid for repeating myself. This time when she answered me she was still crying but was a little more coherent.

"The vest kept rubbing against my nipples. The water…the pain…Jesus, it hurts."

I finally got it. She'd been naked under the life vest, and the constant bobbing up and down in the water must have chafed her nipples raw. "Sshh," I said, stepping into the shower with her. Cozy wasn't the word I'd use to describe the two of us in a one-body shower. Intimate wasn't another, even though Alissa was naked and I wasn't.

"Turn around," I told her, gently putting my hand on her shoulders and turning her so her back was to me. My body was blocking most of the water, which seemed to give her some immediate relief. "Let me help you."

I grabbed the soap and lathered it in my hands, then gently ran them over her back and neck, reaching around to do the same with each of her arms. I repeated the same actions on her legs, staying far enough from her private parts that my mother would be proud.

"Can you wash your chest?" I asked. "It'll probably hurt like hell, but you've got to get the salt water off or you'll never heal."

Alissa nodded, and when I held the soap out in front of her, my chest pressed against her back. Now *that* was intimate.

Her hands shook as she took the bar of soap from me. Lather filled her hands when she handed it back to me. I saw her back stiffen as she ran her hands over her breasts. She moaned, and I think I stopped breathing. I was taller than her so I could see exactly what she was doing over her shoulder. As her hands slid up and down, my heart beat faster. Stop it, I told myself. This woman was simply bathing, not putting on a show for me. God, I felt like a heel for even thinking what my body was telling me to think. Alissa was recovering from a life-and-death situation, and I was leering over her shoulder and lusting at what I was seeing.

Alissa swayed against me, and I caught her before she fell. My arms were wrapped around her waist, and I propped her up against my own body.

"Alissa?" I hoped she hadn't fainted.

"Hurts," she murmured.

"I know. Let's get you rinsed off and into bed. I have some salve we can put on that'll help."

I reached behind me and turned off the water, then slid the towel off the towel bar and wrapped it around her, careful not to cause too much pain as I did. As we stepped out of the shower she sagged against me again. I swept her into my arms and carried her over to my bed. Since I'd just climbed out, the covers were down, the bed probably still warm. I laid her on the sheets still wrapped in the towel, and she started to shiver. I pulled the covers up around her.

"Let me get out of these wet clothes and then I'll get the salve," I said, at the same time pulling my shirt over my head. In a few seconds my sopping-wet clothes were on the floor in the shower and I was dressed in a pair of boxers and an old T-shirt. I searched through the medicine cabinet and finally found what I was looking for, then sat on the edge of the bed. Alissa opened her eyes and looked up at me.

"This will help with the healing," I said, carefully pulling the covers down to her waist. I reached for the end of the towel and stopped. "You'll probably want to do this," I said, holding out the jar and trying not to stammer. Alissa reached for it and I rose off the bed and turned my back, giving her what little privacy I could in the small cabin.

"Put as much of it on as you can stand. It'll soak in in a few minutes."

Alissa groaned and hissed, and as much as I knew I shouldn't, I turned around to check on her. Her sunburned face was pale, her forehead sweating. She was breathing fast, and it looked like she was clenching her teeth. She held the jar out.

"I can't, hurts too much," she said, her voice hoarse. "Just do it, please."

I wasn't sure what she was asking me. To rub this jelly on her breasts? To rub it on her nipples? This was purely medicinal, but holy Christ, what was I going to do?

"Just do it," she repeated softly.

I put two fingers into the jar and swiped out a glob of the stuff. It was the color of Vaseline but smelled like cinnamon. A fisherman's wife had given me a jar eight or nine years ago, and it worked miracles on chapped, weather-beaten skin. And that was exactly how I would describe Alissa's breasts. I took a deep breath.

"Okay, here we go," I said stupidly. Jesus, this wasn't pulling a tooth, but I sure made it sound like one.

The instant my fingers touched her nipples Alissa arched away from me. "Shit, that hurts," she said, several more beads of sweat breaking out on her forehead. "No, don't stop," she demanded. "If you do, I probably won't let you start again."

I hated hurting her but this was exactly what she needed. As gently as I could I smeared the gel over her nipples and areolas. She was breathing fast, in short, shallow gasps.

"Hang on. I'm almost done," I said, trying to reassure her that this agony would end soon. "I need to put some on your arms here." I gently touched the front of her armpit, where the vest had also rubbed her raw and over her sunburned face. Those areas obviously weren't as painful, and her breathing began to return to normal.

"Okay, that should do it for now." This time it was my turn to be hoarse. Playing doctor with a beautiful woman was one thing, but the last few minutes weren't nearly as fulfilling. I stood, wiping my hands on my wet clothes that I'd dropped on the floor. "Give it a few minutes to soak in, and you can put on a T-shirt and get some rest," I murmured. When I looked back at Alissa she was already fast asleep. I tried not to be a voyeur, but I did have to look at her breasts to determine if the gel had penetrated her skin. I winced as I took a good, close-up look. Her nipples were raw, almost oozing. The pain from the salt water must have been unbearable.

I pulled a T-shirt out of the small drawer and tugged it over Alissa's head. She didn't wake when I put her arms through and slid the shirt down her torso. Somehow I managed to pull on a pair of my boxers and added some of the magic gel to what looked like a bite mark on her right calf. It didn't look infected, but I reminded myself to check on it a little later. I pulled the covers up, added another blanket, grabbed a pair of jeans from the drawer, and closed the door behind me.

CHAPTER EIGHT

Bert

I hustled back to the bridge, making sure Blow had marked our coordinates. When Alissa woke and was able to tell us what happened, I'd notify the coast guard. Rock and Limpet were there, along with Blow. "Tell me what happened," I said to him.

He reiterated what little Limpet had said, adding a few more details but not much. He had seen a blinking light in the distance, and even though it would put us off course and schedule, his gut had told him to investigate. He hadn't seen any smoldering debris or sign of a boat. I looked out the windows as if to verify his claim, which was stupid because it was blacker than the bad witch's cape out there. I probably wouldn't have been able to see my hand in front of my face if not for the lights on the *Dream*.

"I just knew something wasn't right." Blow was defending himself. "I know it wasted gas and time, but—"

"It's fine, Blow. You saved her life," I shot back, my nerves finally rising now that the adrenaline had worn off.

"How do you know her?" Rock asked cautiously. I rarely spoke of my personal life while we were out. They all knew I was a lesbian, and once I overheard Hook complain that I got more women than he did. I smiled because it was true. At least at the time. Now I had a hard time remembering the last time I'd kissed a woman, let alone anything else.

"We met at the market on pier fourteen. I was short of cash and she sprung for the difference. We had a cup of coffee later and that was it. It was the night Homeland Security came aboard to ask about the smugglers we saw."

"You must have made quite an impression," Rock said. "Her face sure did light up when she saw you," he added for clarification.

"She was probably scared to death. Not only had she been in the water for God knows how long, but she was rescued by the likes of you three," I said, punching Blow in the arm playfully. This was a serious situation, but it could have been much more. It appeared, at least on the surface, that Alissa was okay, but her boat was another story. We wouldn't be able to see anything until daylight. Not that I expected to. The currents out here were pretty strong.

I was too keyed up to sleep and someone was in my bed, so I took the rest of the night watch, dismissing Blow.

Alissa

My hair was still damp, but I was a lot warmer when I woke than when I lay down. Bert had left me a pair of sweatpants that were a little too long and a flannel shirt that was far too big. A pair of thick, black socks were on my feet. I slid my feet into a pair of old, worn boots next to the bed.

After a few wrong turns I found the bridge. "Permission to come aboard?" I asked weakly from the doorway. My throat was ragged from crying, screaming, smoke, and salt water. It didn't matter which. All that mattered was that I was out of the water. I'd slept a little but woke when a nightmare became a little too vivid.

I'd thought I was going to die. Really and truly going to die. I'd never felt so alone in my life. I'd been alone before, quite a lot, as a matter of fact. I lived alone, traveled alone, and went out on my boat alone. But when I was in the water there was no one.

Absolutely no one. I had no idea how long I'd been there, but it was a lifetime.

I'd thought of my parents, my sisters, my friends, and my employees. How long would it take, if ever, for someone to find my body? Would they think I just left with no word? That I could actually do that? How long would Alissa Cooper Advertising survive? How long until they gave up hope and declared me dead? How long before they could do that—seven years?

My mind had gone to terrible places when I let it, so I'd tried to keep it occupied with good thoughts. I remembered the Christmas when the whole family got bikes and we spent the day riding around the neighborhood. I was eight and quite the show-off, at least until I wasn't paying attention and ran into the light pole. I still have the scar on my knee to prove it. I remembered when I went back to school after a bad bout of the chicken pox in the second grade. I got to wear a sweatshirt and long pants, which was a big deal. I remembered the smile on my sister's face as she walked down the aisle, the fear in her eyes when her baby got sick. The joy in my father's eyes when I graduated from college. My first girlfriend, my first kiss, my first time. I thought of everything to keep my mind away from the present. I was so far out of it I didn't even see Bert's boat until it was practically on top of me.

"Kind of a moot question since you're already here," Bert answered.

God, it was good to hear a voice. "Better late than never," I replied, coughing until I thought I might toss a lung.

"Let's get you something to drink," Bert said, and she took me back to the galley. She put a pot of water on the small stove and pulled a tea bag and a small container of honey from the cupboard.

Every time I tried to say something she shushed me, and it wasn't until I had finished two cups of the soothing tea that she asked, "Feel up to telling me what happened?"

I nodded, pulling the large shirt closer around me, a chill running through my body. "I woke up, smoke everywhere, grabbed a life vest, and jumped." That was the Cliff Notes version, and by the look on Bert's face not what she expected.

"I went to bed around midnight. I'd been out all day and was tired. The mast was down, everything was buttoned down, and my running lights were on. I checked and double-checked everything like I always do and set the perimeter alarm before turning in." Admittedly I was a bit OCD when it came to that procedure. "I secured the stateroom door, climbed into bed, pulled up the covers, and fell asleep almost instantly. The next thing I knew the smoke detector was screaming, and when I opened the door, smoke poured in." A tremor ran through me as I remembered the acrid smell of the smoke, and I fought down a cough.

"The entire galley and main cabin were engulfed in flames. I grabbed a life vest from under the bed, shimmied out the porthole above my bed, and jumped. I swam for several minutes to get away, the heat from the flames intense, and with all the fuel on board and the propane tanks in the galley, I thought it would explode any minute. Somehow I got into the life vest, activated the emergency beacon, and that's it. She went down in minutes." In all actuality it had happened just about as fast as I recounted it, and my voice cracked on the last few words.

I remembered watching her sink and thinking of the scene in the movie *Titanic* when the survivors watched in horror as the greatest ship in the world slowly drifted under the frigid waters. *Adventures* wasn't quite so elegant. It just burned down to the fiberglass hull and then silently sank into the dark water.

Bert looked at her watch and frowned.

"What time is it?" I asked.

"Six fifteen," she said, almost apologetically. We picked you up at one forty."

"What day is it?"

"Thursday."

"Thursday?" Holy shit. I'd been in the water almost forty-eight hours. No wonder I was totally exhausted.

"What day did you think it was?"

"I had no idea. When I went to bed it was Tuesday."

"And you were out alone?" Bert asked.

"Yes."

"This far out?"

"Yes."

"Alone?"

Now I was mad. My nerves were shot, I was completely exhausted, and my throat felt like sandpaper. "Yes, alone," I snapped. "All alone, just me, myself, and I," I added sarcastically.

"Do you often go out by yourself?"

"Yes, I do." I was getting angrier. I expected for the coast guard to question me, but not for a tuna-boat captain to grill me. "I'm a seasoned sailor with over twenty years on the water and have never run into any trouble."

"Great way to start," Bert said with her own sarcasm. "What was your boat?"

"She's a…" I stopped. That was present tense. I need to shift to past tense. "She was a thirty-nine-foot sailboat with a forty-horsepower engine. She had a beam of thirteen one and eight hundred square feet of mast. She held forty gallons of fuel and one hundred of water." I provided all the specs because Bert obviously knew her boats, and I wasn't about to let her think I was a stupid rookie on the water. Judging by the way she nodded and quirked her lips, I knew I'd succeeded.

"I need to report this to the coast guard," Bert said officially. "What was the name and number of your boat?"

I recited the particulars, and Bert wrote them down in a small black book. "Would you like to use the radio to call home?"

I thought for a minute. "Nobody to call at this hour."

Bert looked at me, a question on her face. "Nobody's missing you?"

"No. I'm not due back into port until Sunday."

I couldn't read Bert's expression. Finally she asked, "Will you be okay for a few minutes?"

"Sure. Go on and do what you need to do. I'll have another cup if I don't drop over from exhaustion." It wouldn't surprise me if, the instant Bert left, I laid my head on the table in front of me and fell asleep instantly.

"Since we're all up I'm fixing breakfast," a man said and started puttering around the galley. My stomach growled loudly. He held out his hand. It was stained, and he was missing the end of his right index finger.

"My name is Francis, but people call me Lefty."

"Pleased to meet you, Lefty."

"Can I get you some coffee?" he asked in a slow Southern drawl.

"Yes, that would be nice, thank you."

"How do you like your eggs, Miss Cooper?" he asked.

"Please, call me Alissa. Um…" I hesitated. "Scrambled?" I asked, not sure this really was a short-order kitchen.

"Scrambled eggs in five," he said, turning back toward the stove and reaching for two eggs in the container to his left.

I was still coming to grips with my situation when two of the men I recognized as my rescuers came in.

"Good morning," I said.

"You scared us pretty good, ma'am," the scrawny man to my left said. He looked incredibly familiar but I couldn't place him.

"Have we met?" I asked, wracking my brain to remember how I knew him.

"No, ma'am. I would have remembered. You're way out of my league."

"You got that right, Limpet," the man to his right said. He held out a big, beefy hand with a pristine white bandage around his thumb.

"Rock, nice to meet you. This sap here is called Limpet." He nodded to the scrawny man. "What's your real name by the way, Limpet?"

"Roger," the man said, the name obviously distasteful coming out of his mouth.

Then I realized who he looked like. I almost said so but didn't want to insult my hosts. But there was no need when Limpet stated the obvious.

"Everybody says I look like that old-time actor Don Knotts when he played in the movie *The Incredible Mr. Limpet.*"

"I can definitely see the resemblance," I said, relaxing a little. An industrial thick, white ceramic coffee cup was placed in front of me along with a twelve-inch plastic dinner plate, no less than half of it filled with a heaping pile of scrambled eggs, the other half with golden-brown hash browns and five strips of crispy, thick bacon hanging off the edge. Talk about food overdose, I thought, looking at the plate in front of me.

"Dig in," Limpet said, getting his own plate. "It's a long time till lunch."

❖

The food smelled delicious, and my empty stomach echoed the thought. My hands were still shaking when I reached for the salt and pepper, but not nearly as much as they had when I first came aboard. I wasn't warm, but the chill had abated a bit so it was probably delayed shock.

When I was in the water I'd more or less been calm and clearheaded and conserved my energy. I had no idea if I'd be found before or after I died, or ever. I suppose I should have panicked or freaked out, but I didn't. Now it was setting in just how close I'd been to dying, and the adrenaline was starting to wane. I would crash in a few minutes.

"I notified the coast guard," Bert said as she came back in. She sat down across from me, her face serious. Shit, what now?

"They're tied up with a storm off the coast of Florida, and since you're not injured you'll stay with us till they can get here or we arrive back in port."

"How long will that be?"

"They said they'd get here as soon as they can."

"Can you take me in?"

"No, I'm sorry, but we can't."

"I'll pay you." I ventured what I thought was a good compromise.

"I'm sorry, but you can't afford me."

"You don't have any idea what I can or can't afford," I shot back.

"Sorry, no. First of all, there's a storm behind us I don't want to go through again, and second, we've been out six days and won't reach our fishing area for another four or five. I can't afford to lose the time to take you back."

I looked around and, along with Lefty, I knew at least three other men were on board, as well as Bert, whom I knew very little about. Quite disturbing, if I do say so myself. I must have given myself away because Bert said, "You'll be all right here. You can use the ship-to-shore phone to call." She hesitated and looked at my naked ring finger. "You can let whoever you need to know you're okay and won't be back for a few weeks."

"A few weeks! Are you kidding me?" I know I sounded ungrateful to the people who'd saved my life, but I couldn't stay on this boat for that long. Bert's expression told me she thought so too.

"I'm afraid so. That's if we don't run into any problems," Bert said calmly.

Her explanation made sense and I did the math, but I still couldn't stay on the boat for a month. "I have obligations, a job, and people depending on me. Client presentations," I said, listing just a few of my To Do's.

"I do too," Bert replied quickly but firmly. "If we don't work we don't get paid. Every one of my guys depends on me for his paycheck. There's no paid time off. We can't reschedule the season. You can reschedule a meeting."

"You mean you won't." I realized that I sounded more than a little snarky. If I wasn't so tired I might be a little more diplomatic. Who was this woman who refused to turn around and take me back? Where in the fuck was the coast guard? Wasn't that what I paid taxes for?

"In this case they're one and the same."

"But—"

"No," Bert said firmly.

The way she'd shut me down really pissed me off. I detected something in her eyes but obviously didn't know her well enough to understand what it meant. It could have been regret or it could have been victory. I thought about hiring someone to come and get me, but it would probably cost an arm and a leg. Even if I could find someone, no one would come this far out with the storms brewing around us. Either way I wasn't going anywhere for far longer than I'd like. And I hoped not an hour longer. I stifled a yawn, too tired to argue about this issue anymore.

"Let's get you to bed," Bert said. "You look like you could sleep standing up." She stood and put her dishes and mine in the sink. "Come on. You can stay in my cabin."

I had no choice but to follow her. She was the captain and I was completely exhausted.

CHAPTER NINE

Alissa

I looked around Bert's cabin. It was small, about eight feet by ten, and contained the single bed behind me, a small desk, and a dresser. In the corner was what looked like a MacBook tucked into one of the cubbies. The contents of each cubby were secured with a screen, snapped tight to keep the items from spilling out in rough seas. A reading light was clipped to the edge of the desk, and a few papers lay scattered across the top. A floor-to-ceiling bureau stood to one side, flanked on either side by square windows.

A few framed pictures adorned the walls, and even as exhausted as I was I had an overwhelming need to know more about the woman who would control my life for the next few weeks. In one photo Bert was standing with her arms around a man that could only be her father, the resemblance unmistakable. Judging by the smile on their faces and the dimples in both cheeks, I had little doubt who the man was and even less doubt that they loved each other. In another was a little girl, obviously Bert, who looked about four or five years old. She was holding a fishing pole twice her size in one hand, and a fish equally big was hanging from a hook to the left. I don't know much about fishing, but I gathered it might have been the first fish she ever caught. The other photos showed Bert with other people, and in all of them her smile was dazzling.

Exhaustion finally drove me to the bed, and I crawled between the covers. They were warm and smelled of sea air and Bert. The pillow was soft, but when I laid my head down my mind started racing.

My body started to shake when the enormity of my situation hit. I could have died. I could have succumbed to smoke inhalation, drowning, or the fire itself. If Bert and her crew hadn't found me, I would have. I might have lasted another two or three days at most but no longer than that. What in the hell had happened? I'd checked everything before I turned in and found no indication anything was amiss. Jesus, by the time I woke, the whole boat was engulfed. Holy shit.

Luck didn't even begin to describe Bert's boat finding me. I believe in God, or at least something bigger than me, and he or she or it must have been watching out for me. Why? Did I have some unfinished business? To touch someone in a meaningful, life-altering way? Whatever the reason, I was more than a little grateful.

After Ariel, many days I'd thought I'd die of humiliation or pain, or that the anger would eat me up. But I'd never wished I would die. I must admit, though, that the idea crossed my mind more than once when I was in the water. I suppose it wasn't my turn.

The last few days had ravaged my body and my mind, but my thoughts kept jumping around. I was saved but was I safe? I was on a ship in the middle of the ocean with eight people I didn't know, six of them men. That thought certainly didn't calm the voices in my head. No one was expecting me for several days, and I could be all the way around the world by then in some godforsaken country sold into white slavery.

"Jesus Christ, Alissa, can you make it any worse?" I said, my voice weak and raspy, my throat hurting. I forced my wildly creative imagination to stop and focus on what I did know.

Bert appeared to be a respectable businesswoman. The people in the café knew her and seemed to genuinely like her. I didn't get any weird vibes from her or from any of her crew I'd met so far. I trusted my gut and felt my nerves start to settle. I'd been scared shitless, but now I needed to get my arms around the situation. I was smart and resourceful and could think fast on my feet. I just needed to rest.

I closed my eyes and the room began to spin. I immediately opened them, gripped the sheet, and tried to focus. An old-fashioned Big Ben alarm clock about the size of my palm sat on a table next to the bed, and I concentrated on the second hand as it moved around the dial. I forced my body to relax and tried to block everything from my mind except the soft tick, tick, tick as the thin hand passed over each number and the four lines between them.

CHAPTER TEN

Bert

"What the fuck?" I hustled the remaining ten steps to my cabin door. A second scream pierced the stillness, and I turned the knob and stepped inside, not knowing what I'd find. I trusted my crew and knew they wouldn't hurt Alissa. She was lying on her back in my bed, her arms and legs moving as if she were treading water. The covers were off and my T-shirt had slid up, exposing her stomach. It was tan, and she obviously was able to do more than a few dozen crunches.

She moaned, tossing her head back and forth, and becoming more agitated. I sat down on the side of the bed, and before I could grab her hands, one of them hit the left side of my face. Stars danced behind my eyes for a moment, and when they stopped spinning I grabbed her arms and pulled them to my chest. Leaning over her I said her name quietly. "Alissa." When she didn't respond I repeated it a little louder.

"Alissa, you're having a dream. Alissa, you're safe. You're on my boat, you're safe." When she didn't wake I crawled into the bed beside her and pulled her into my arms. She fought me, but I held her tight and repeated over and over again that she was safe. Finally, after a few minutes, she stopped trembling and settled into me. Her breathing returned to the deep in-and-out of sleep and I relaxed.

She smelled like ocean and sunshine. Her hair was tangled, but I gradually sorted through it with my fingers. She lay quietly, settling down.

A soft knock on my door startled me. I'd been daydreaming of another place, another time, where the actuality of Alissa asleep in my arms was possible, and I looked down to see that she was still asleep. "Come in," I said, my voice a little more than a whisper.

Blow stuck just his head inside. "Captain?" He blushed and stammered, "Oh shit, I'm sorry. I thought you said come in." He started to back out of the doorway.

"It's all right," I said a little louder, stopping his retreat. "She was having a nightmare. What do you need?" I hoped he'd say nothing, but he didn't hear my prayers.

"Lefty sent me down to tell you chow will be ready in about fifteen minutes." His eyes darted everywhere except to Alissa and me on my bed.

"Thanks. I'll be right there." I didn't want to move from where I was, but we had a schedule to keep and I was the captain. Slowly, so as not to wake Alissa, I shifted. Alissa jerked, obviously startled.

"Sshh," I said. "It's all right. You're safe. It's Bert and you're on my boat. You're safe," I repeated until she relaxed. Her hand was on my chest, her legs intertwined with mine like lovers often do.

"What time is it?" she asked, her voice weak.

I turned my head, but my awkward position prevented me from seeing the clock. "Time to eat," I said instead. She shifted, and for a moment I thought of holding her so she couldn't leave my arms. But I thought better of it and let her go.

Alissa sat up and ran her hand through her hair, pushing it off her face. She was sunburned, but not burned nearly as bad as she could have been if not for her obvious hours in the sun. She looked at me, then around the room, then back at me. Her eyes started to blaze.

"You were having a nightmare," I said to her unasked question. "This was the only thing that calmed you down." I could see she was still skeptical.

"Look," I said, climbing out of the bed. "I realize you don't know me from Adam, but I am not going to take advantage of this situation. You are a guest on this boat, and my crew and I will treat you as one. You're safe here," I said, waving my hand around the room. "From everyone."

"But you won't take me back? I'm your prisoner."

"No, you're not a prisoner. You're not confined anywhere, but when we reach our fishing area you'll need to stay out of the way."

"Or what?"

"Or I will lock you up."

"You can't do that."

"Yes, I can and I will. The safety of everyone on this boat is my responsibility, and I take it very seriously. If that's what it takes…"

A flicker of something passed over Alissa's face, then disappeared. "Okay. Now that we've settled that, let's get you something to eat. You'll feel better with some food and drink in you. Then you can come back and turn in for the night if you'd like."

Alissa moved off the bed, her legs buckling beneath her. I was able to catch her before she slid to the floor and pulled her back onto the bed.

"I'm fine," she barked, brushing my hand away.

"Maybe you should lie down again. I'll go get something and bring it to you."

"No," she said abruptly. "I just need to get my sea legs. Give me a minute."

Against my better judgment I gave her a few, and this time when she stood up she stayed that way.

"See," she said sarcastically. "I'm fine."

She still looked a little wobbly to me but I wasn't going to argue. Instead I took her arm and led her out the door.

❖

Alissa

By the time we reached the galley, I was a little steadier on my feet. When I sat down at the table, Lefty placed a heaping portion of spaghetti in front of me. He did the same for Bert, then returned to his chair next to Limpet. Looking around the table I didn't see the other two guys whose names I didn't remember, which meant they were probably manning the helm, keeping us on course. But then again I really had no idea what they were doing.

"Looks delicious," I said, reaching for a fork in the center of the table. Conversation around me picked up again, and from what I could tell the men were discussing the recent fight between two heavyweight boxers. I recognized the names, having worked with the World Boxing Federation preparing some collateral material for the bout. The WBF was trying to appeal to more female fans and thought a female ad agency would help in that effort. As part of my payment I received two seats to the event, nine rows back from the ring.

"It was a great fight," I said. Five pairs of eyes looked at me. "What? It was a great fight."

"You watched it?" Limpet asked.

"Yes," I replied, not including just how close I was when I did so.

"Awesome," Limpet said, obviously in awe.

"Can you tell me again exactly what happened?" Bert asked, drawing my attention back to her.

"Montoya came out swinging right from the start. He has a nasty right uppercut and when—"

"What are you talking about?" Bert asked.

"The fight."

"What fight?"

"The fight you just asked me about."

"What?" Bert asked again, obviously confused. "No, I was asking about your boat."

"My boat? I already told you."

"I'd like to hear it again," she said calmly. "You may have forgotten something."

"What is there to forget? Everything was fine, I went to bed, I woke up, my boat was on fire, and I jumped. You rescued me, end of incident."

"You don't remember anything else?"

My patience expired. "If I did I'd tell you. Do you think I'm lying?"

"Are you?"

"Of course not," I said firmly.

"Then there's no problem."

"Only one, and that is that I'm stuck on this boat. I don't have time for this."

"And I don't have time to take you back. Since this is my boat and I'm the captain, I win."

❖

Alissa

"Why don't you turn in? You still look pretty thrashed," Bert said, eyeing me critically. We'd finished dinner but hadn't gotten up from the table. "You'd probably feel much better after a good night's sleep."

I hate being told what to do, and no way was my jailer going to. "What are you going to do?"

"I'll take the watch for a while," Bert replied.

"I'll come along." I made it a statement, not a request.

Bert raised her eyebrows, obviously surprised. At this point I didn't care what she thought. I'd almost died, and it was all about me right now. I'm not normally this selfish, but damn it, I'd earned it.

"Suit yourself," Bert replied, seeming somewhat unsure, then left the galley. I guess I was on my own to get to the bridge.

Once on the bridge I sat down in the chair to Bert's left. It was quiet for several minutes, or at least as quiet as it could be with forty tons of steel and rigging moving through the ocean. The rhythmic motion as the big vessel churned through the water was familiar and soothing.

"How long have you been fishing?" I asked, trying to regain control of the conversation.

"I caught my first fish when I was four."

I remembered the picture on the wall in her cabin. "And now you're the captain of your own ship."

"Well, there were a few steps in between," Bert said flatly.

I hated a smart-ass. "Tell me."

"Tell you what?"

"Tell me about the steps in between."

"All of them?"

"It's not like we're going anywhere for the next few weeks," I said.

"I'm glad to see you have your sense of humor back."

"Yeah, well, that's all I have left from this trip. I don't even have a pair of underwear." Or my boat that cost three hundred and sixty thousand dollars, I thought.

Bert laughed and the sound filled the room. "You were about to tell me your fish tales." I felt an odd fluttering in my stomach.

"Fish tales?"

"Yes, the stories about all the fish you've caught."

"They're not really that exciting," Bert replied.

"I'll be the judge of that," I said. Bert looked at me for a few moments. I had no idea what she was looking for, and it made me nervous.

"How about we swap?"

"Swap?" I was confused.

"Yeah, I tell you one, you tell me one."

I thought about that proposal for a few moments. What the hell? "I can do that. When did you get your first boat?"

"I was twelve. I saved all my Christmas and birthday money and all my allowance and bought a ten-foot rowboat. It needed some work but the transom was solid. You?"

"Fourteen. She was a twelve-foot sailboat my neighbor had neglected for years. It was sitting in his backyard under a tarp, and when he died his wife gave it to me. She said she was finally getting it out of her yard."

"College?"

"Smith. You?" As soon as the words came out of my mouth I knew better. Bert was a fisherman. She wouldn't have gone to college.

"Boston College."

I felt my mouth embarrassingly drop open.

"You're surprised," Bert said

I managed to clamp my mouth shut, then opened it. "I just assumed." My excuse was stupid, my ignorance blatant.

"I was a dumb fisherman," Bert said. I detected a hint of bitterness in her tone.

"Absolutely not." I defended myself. "I never thought that." I don't think she believed me.

"Yep, summa cum laude, class of 2000. Your turn," Bert said.

"How did you get into commercial fishing?"

"I come from a long line of fishermen. My first memory was standing on the captain's chair on my grandfather's boat so I could see over the wheel." Bert smiled. Obviously it was a fond memory.

"I'll bet you were a handful."

"My mother would agree. I was the only girl, and she wanted me to be frilly and girly and love to cook like she did. I just wanted to be outside or on the boat with my dad or grandfather. I was six when I went on my first overnight. I was on my best behavior for weeks so my mom would let me go. I had to promise to stay out of the way and do exactly as I was told. It was one of the best trips of my life."

Even though I couldn't make out her face in the dark, I heard a smile in her voice as she led me down her memory lane.

"So tell me about advertising."

Bert's question took me out of my thoughts and straight to Ariel. I immediately became defensive and cautious. "Why do you want to know?"

Bert looked at me before she answered. "Because you asked me about my job. Now I'm asking you about yours."

I had to stop being so suspicious. Not everyone's an Ariel. But I'd missed it the first time, so who's to say I'd catch it the second? "I started my firm eight years ago after my boss stole one too many of my ideas. I had some money stashed away and rented a storefront at Belton Avenue and Thirty-second Street. I put together my portfolio and pounded the pavement. I still have my first customer and a few more," I said.

"If you had a thirty-nine-foot Catalina, I venture to say you've had more than a few more clients. But it's none of my business," Bert added quickly.

"A few." Bert was right. It was none of her business.

"So how is it a successful, beautiful woman doesn't have someone at home waiting for her?"

"Maybe I don't want some*one*," I replied. Bert looked at me. "I'm not a player. Just been there, done that, will never go there again."

"Ouch, sounds painful."

"No, just ugly." I surprised myself by saying that much. Bert was practically a stranger and I kept my personal life, well, personal.

"Sorry about that," Bert said softly.

"No need to apologize," I said. "It's over, no need to look back." Except every year when the parole hearing rolled around. I wondered if the board had made its decision yet. Typically it sent a standard form letter a few weeks after the hearing. Paul should be receiving it any day. I could use the ship-to-shore radio and call him and find out, but I had enough to deal with. I didn't need the thought of Ariel walking the streets again. Nothing I could do about it anyway.

"Same question to you. Aren't captains supposed to have their pick of fair young maidens in each port?" I asked.

"Who says I don't?" was Bert's quick reply.

"Touché," I said and gave her a small salute.

"Actually the *Dream* has only one port, and that's Colton Harbor. So anyone I leave behind is still there when I get home."

"Ah, so you don't leave a trail of broken hearts?"

Bert laughed again. "I let my guys do that. I don't give myself that much credit. That and it's hard to develop any kind or relationship when you're gone as much as I am."

"How often do you go out?"

"Depends. Some trips last a few days, and others are long like this one. Depends on the weather, the fish, and a whole bunch of things."

"How long have you had this boat?"

"Seven years."

"Would you do it all over again?"

"In a heartbeat," Bert answered just as quickly. "It's what I've always wanted."

"And now you have it."

"And now I have it," she replied, contentment in her voice.

"What's next?"

"Depends."

"On?"

"This catch."

"What's so special about this catch?"

"If it's successful, I'll have what I need to buy a few things to make improvements."

"And I'm stuck out here for 'a few things'?" Bert didn't answer. "Like what?"

Bert proceeded to rattle off a list, and from what I could gather, it was pretty impressive. Some of it I didn't understand and she patiently explained. She had big plans for expansion and efficiency.

"So why were you out here in the middle of nowhere alone?"

Unlike the first time she asked the question, this time she sounded curious instead of accusatory, but it was still a sore spot.

"It clears my head."

"I know what you mean," Bert said simply.

"Do you ever take anyone along?"

Was she fishing—pardon the pun—to find out if I ever brought a woman along? "Not often," I answered honestly. "Entertaining makes it difficult to clear my head."

"True, but there are lots of ways to clear your head."

Was Bert flirting with me? In any other circumstance I'd say yes, but I was still off my game a bit. I also couldn't see her face or eyes because it was too dark. I'm a good reader of people—well, with the exception of Ariel. I chided myself to stop using Ariel as a reference point for everything.

It had been like that in the beginning after she left. I suppose it's like that for most abrupt endings to a relationship. Ariel loved that Italian restaurant. That was Ariel's favorite movie. Ariel pushed the shopping cart like this. Ariel had invaded my psyche like an enemy, and ultimately my self-confidence. Repairing it was obviously still a work in progress.

CHAPTER ELEVEN

Bert

When I was on the bridge I preferred to be alone. Alissa had described it perfectly when she said being on the water cleared her head. It gave me a sense of calm and peace I've never found anywhere else. The solitude, no one between me, God, and the sea. It was humbling.

Unlike my peers, I often took the night watch. I couldn't work every night; I have to be sharp and alert when we're casting or retrieving the nets. But we wouldn't be at our fishing location for another few days. Plenty of time to take a few shifts and catch a few hours of sleep. And thinking about sleep, Alissa had been quiet for some time. When I looked at her, her eyes were closed.

I'd often thought about what I would do if I found myself in Alissa's situation. Stranded in the middle of nowhere, the only hope of rescue a sheer miracle. I've had hours of survival training, but I always wondered how I would fare if faced with what Alissa had experienced.

I hoped I would be mentally and emotionally strong. Physically, I think I'd do okay. Years of hard work had made me fit and strong. How would I feel if I knew I was going to die? Would I pray? Scream? Cry? Would I give up hope?

A cool breeze floated into the bridge when Blow opened the door. I looked at Alissa, who had fallen asleep earlier. Even though strands of hair blew across her face, she didn't stir.

"How's it going, Cap?" Blow asked, setting a thermos of coffee on the counter behind me.

"Quiet," I replied. He was here to relieve me and I suddenly felt very tired. It had been a long, busy, stressful day, and if I'd be battling Alissa again all day tomorrow, it would be a doubly long day.

"Wake me if you stumble upon any more women floating in the ocean," I joked.

I turned to Alissa. I didn't want to wake her but she couldn't spend the night here. I touched her arm lightly. "Alissa." Her eyes opened slowly, and for a few moments a look of panic filled them. I stepped into her line of sight and it quickly disappeared.

"Hey," I said, keeping my tone light. "Now it's really time for you to get some sleep. Come on." I touched her elbow and pulled her to her feet.

"I'm—"

"I know. You're fine. Good, let's go."

Silently, Alissa followed me down three flights of narrow, metal stairs and through the hall to my cabin. I felt her eyes on me the entire time, but she didn't say anything. When we reached my cabin I opened the door and motioned her to go in first.

"I'd offer you another shower, but I'm afraid we limit ourselves to only one a day. Captain's orders."

"And you're the boss," she said stiffly, definitely not in awe of my position.

"I'm just trying to do what's right for the crew and the boat."

"Obviously."

"Breakfast is at six, but sleep as long as you'd like. It's just another day at sea, with nothing to do till we reach the fishing ground."

"Where are you going to sleep?"

"I'll crash in the galley."

"I'm kicking you out of your bed."

"I'll be fine," I said, lying with my fingers crossed behind my back. No way would I get any sleep on those chairs, but I refused to tell Alissa that.

"I'll sleep somewhere else."

"There is nowhere else. Unless you want to bunk with the guys." A look I couldn't recognize washed across her face. I think it was a combination of panic, fear, and uncertainty. "Don't be a martyr. Just get in," I said, my patience thin and my body tired. She hesitated a few moments, then stepped inside.

"You can sleep with me. It'll be a tight squeeze but I don't mind."

I hesitated, not knowing exactly what to say.

"Don't be a martyr, Bert. Just come in," she said, repeating my words.

"Something wrong?" she asked after we'd both used the bathroom to get ready.

"Uh, no," I replied weakly. I just wasn't sure how you go about platonically sharing a bed with someone who doesn't really like you. And there was no mistake how she felt about me.

"Get over it and get in," Alissa said, finally spurring me out of my stupor and into action.

"Okay. I'm not going to turn down an offer to join a beautiful woman in my own bed." I was trying to ease the tension from her face. When she smiled I saw a flash of relief pass over her lovely features.

"Inside or outside?" Alissa asked, pointing to the bed.

"Outside," I replied. "If I'm needed in the night I won't wake you getting out." When Alissa pushed the sweatpants down her hips I tried real hard not to look. I failed miserably. She was wearing a pair of my boxers and looked just plain sexy. I pulled my boots off, tossed my jeans on the chair, and slid into bed beside her.

I didn't remember it being this cozy, but then again we were now both wide-awake and completely aware of where we were.

Alissa shifted a little, her bare leg touched mine, and a fire shot up my leg and smoldered in the pit of my stomach. Oh, dear, this was not a good idea. If I thought I wouldn't get any sleep in the galley, I sure as hell wouldn't get any with Alissa and her bare legs pressing against me. Even though she was being a bitch toward me, I'm still a living, breathing lesbian.

I hugged the side of the bed, not trusting myself to get too close. I hadn't moved since I pulled the covers up, and I'd never felt as uncomfortable as I did right now. God, give me strength, I repeated to myself several times.

"For God's sake, Bert, scoot over," she said. "You're about to fall off."

Better than falling into you, I thought. I did as she asked, and after a few more adjustments we finally settled in. I don't know how long we lay there, neither of us sleeping. My mind was racing with thoughts of what I'd rather be doing with Alissa in my bed, and staring at the ceiling wasn't one of them.

"Go to sleep," she said.

Yeah, right. The only way that was going to happen was if the last few days had never occurred. My body was far too aware of how long it had been since I'd had a woman lying beside me, and one as charming and beautiful as Alissa only exacerbated my reaction. Why couldn't Alissa be the type of woman I despised? Better yet, someone I felt only friendship for. Why did she have to ignite the spark of desire not only because of her fabulous body but her sharp mind as well?

The throbbing between my legs convinced me that at this moment, what was in her brain wasn't at the top of my get-to-know-Alissa priority list. I tried to make myself feel like a cad for lusting after her but gave up. My nerves were shot, and all I could think about was that she was going to be this close for the next few weeks. I squeezed my eyes shut and tried to pretend I was somewhere else.

CHAPTER TWELVE

Alissa

This nightmare was worse than the first one. I'm in the water, the waves churning angrily around me. My life vest is keeping my head above the waves, and I thank God I was aware enough to grab it on my way out. I spin around a complete three hundred sixty degrees, and the scenery doesn't change. My boat is nowhere in sight, nor is land or anything other than dark skies and choppy water. I fight down panic as I realize my situation. I'm going to die. I am going to die. My body will never be found. My boat had burned and sunk without a sound hours ago. At least I thought it was hours ago. It was some time during the night when I bailed overboard, but with no watch and the sun not yet peeking above the horizon, I have no idea how long I've been in the water.

I'm glad I went to the gym regularly and even more thankful for all the miles I swam in the pool. I'm a strong swimmer, but as I look around I have no idea which direction to go. Even if I knew, the current will dictate my ending location, not my breast stroke. I can't do anything but wait. Wait to be rescued, wait to be eaten by a shark, wait to die of exposure.

I'm afraid to close my eyes, fearing I'll miss a boat or a rescue plane nearby. My eyeballs are almost as fried as my face. The reflection of the sun off the water has burned my face, and my lips are raw and swollen. The constant splashing of the waves against my fried skin exacerbates my condition. The pain is almost unbearable, but as long as it hurts, I'm still alive.

I'm exhausted, and as much as I want to drift off, I don't dare. In addition to keeping watch for someone to rescue me, I'm afraid if I do, I'll never open them again. Occasionally something brushes against my leg and I frantically look around for a fin.

In addition to being completely alone, helpless, and terrified, I'm totally naked. I was in such a hurry to get off my burning boat I made one stop, and that was for my life vest. As the sun moved across the sky and the hours passed, it definitely proved to be the best decision I'd ever made. I don't even mind too much that the rough material has rubbed my nipples raw. I don't even want to imagine what the salt water is doing to the other delicate parts of my body.

I sing every song I know and make up the words I don't. I recite the names and physical descriptions of every teacher, friend, and girlfriend I've ever had. I revisit every vacation spot I've ever spent time in, all in an attempt to retain my sanity. If I don't keep my mind busy I'll soon start counting angels.

God, my head is pounding. I'm thirsty and cold. Miles and miles of water, and if I drink any of it I'll die a miserable death. I remember reading an article that explained that because the kidneys are the filters for our waste they can only make urine that is less salty than salt water. Since sea water has more salt than regular water, the more you drink, the more the kidneys have to use existing water from our body in order to dilute the extra salt, which in turn makes us feel even thirstier. Ironically the more salt water you drink, the thirstier you become until you ultimately die from dehydration.

I must have dozed off because when I wake the sun has dipped below the horizon. Frantically I look around and cry when the view is no different than it was when I jumped overboard. I guess my body is compensating for the lack of water because I have no tears, and dry sobs wrack my body. I try to scream, but with my parched throat I can't manage anything more than a croak. If I do spot a ship, how am I going to signal it? I certainly can't catch anyone's attention by yelling. I suddenly remember the blinking white light attached to the shoulder of my life vest. It can be seen during the day and is even more visible in the dark, which increases my chances of rescue. I can think of only one problem: someone has to be looking for it.

I watch the stars as they make their entrance into the dark sky. I search for the Big Dipper, Pisces, and Pegasus. I'm a bit of an astronomy buff and used to often spend hours on my boat lying on my back, the peaceful night sky washing away the clutter in my mind. Hours would slide by as I listened to the gentle slap of waves against the hull. Some mornings I woke to the early daylight rays of the sun slowly replacing the stars.

This would have been one of those nights, but it is anything but peaceful. I'm not a particularly religious person. I believe there is something greater than I am and the body is just a vessel for the soul. When the body dies, the soul is set free like a butterfly with wings. I'd always envisioned my death to be peaceful, preferably on my boat surrounded by friends and family as I cast out to sea. However, I didn't expect it to be quite this soon and certainly not like this.

I scream when something bites my leg. I kick wildly to scare it away, then think better of it. My flailing might make me look more like a tasty morsel than I already do. Whatever bit me wasn't big enough to be a shark. That particular predator would have bitten my entire leg off. However, the stinging in my calf clearly indicates that whatever it was has definitely broken the skin. I hope it isn't bleeding too much or the next bite might be my last.

As more stars appear I start getting philosophical. Does everyone reflect on their life when they're closest to death? It's not like we have the chance to go back and do it again. Shouldn't we take time at various intervals in our lives to be able to course correct, if necessary, before it's too late? Is this my chance?

It certainly didn't look like it. If I weren't dead by morning I'd certainly be by this time tomorrow. No way would I survive another day exposed to the blistering sun.

I close my eyes, the flashing beacon penetrating my eyelids. My heart beats in time with the pulsating light. Is this what death is like? All the stars lining up? There is a certain rhythm when you're born, and there must be when you die.

I keep my eyes closed, remembering happier times. The time my dad taught me how to ride a bike. My first car, first crush, first kiss. The day I signed the lease on the building that would house my company. The day I opened my doors for business. The first Alissa Cooper business card. I'm proud of my life, my accomplishments, and my contribution to society.

A face flashes across my eyelids. It has short, dark hair, blistering green eyes, and deep dimples. The smile lights up her entire face. Bert. Circumstances cut our meeting short, and even though I'd considered that a good thing, much to my annoyance, I'd thought of her quite a few times since. I knew with the whole law thing that I should steer clear, and it pissed me off that I didn't want to. But the episode with Ariel had taught me to ignore the "want" and stick with the practical, sure thing—calculated, fact-based actions.

I drift off and don't fight it. I'm exhausted and whatever will be will be. At this point it's up to something and someone greater than I am. I'm in their hands. With one last look in the sky, I close my eyes.

I feel myself being pulled upward toward heaven and am at peace. Suddenly the smooth movements turn jerky as I'm lifted out of the water. I cough when my life vest digs into my throat. I open my eyes, completely disoriented. People are shouting, hands are grabbing my arms and legs, unbuckling my life vest. I cry out when cool air hits my raw, wet skin. Voices are talking, but my mind is so foggy I can't make out what they're saying.

"Alissa, Alissa." The voice tries to penetrate the fog that has enveloped me. "Alissa."

Bert's voice cuts through my nightmare and I open my eyes. She's leaning over me, concern written all over her face. I can't catch my breath; my dream scared the shit out of me.

"Alissa, you're okay, you're safe," Bert said, obviously trying to reassure me.

She has to repeat her reassurances a few more times before I finally begin to settle down. My heart's racing and I'm covered in sweat. Bert gathers me in her arms. I'm safe, and that's all that matters.

❖

I can't go back to sleep so I replay the events of two nights ago. After dinner I took a glass filled with three fingers of Crown over ice and sat in the deck chair at the rear of my boat. This was my favorite time of the day when I was on the water. The day was winding down, the air crisp and quiet. With each passing minute I felt myself relax more and more. It was the end of my third day out, and I was finally starting to feel like myself again. I knew seeing Ariel would be difficult, but I had totally underestimated the effect. Being in her presence completely threw me. I thought I was over it and her and had moved on, but the anger and betrayal that flooded me told me otherwise. Would I ever recover from her? No, I'd never get over what she did, but hopefully someday I would put it in the right place in my brain and move on.

It must have been close to midnight when I climbed out of the chair and started making my rounds. I followed the same routine every time I pulled in or out of my slip and when I anchored for the night. I double-checked the bow and stern anchor and made sure my sails were secured and that no loose lines were lying around. I secured the chair I'd been sitting in and took the key out of the ignition. I checked the cabin hatch, locking it from the inside, and locked the windows. I hadn't used the stove or oven on this trip, but I checked that the propane valve was in the off position. The coffee pot was unplugged and all the water off. I checked the clip on my 9mm and laid it back on the nightstand—a girl can't be too careful. Then I stripped down to what God gave me on my birthday and slid under the covers. The next thing I knew my boat was on fire and I was jumping over the side.

"What are you thinking about?"

Bert's voice surprised me. "Now that my mind is a little clearer, I was just trying to figure out what happened."

"Have you?" Bert's voice rumbled in her chest under my ear.

"No," I answered, frustrated. "I have a routine…" I proceeded to walk through it with her. Bert asked a few clarifying questions but otherwise stayed quiet.

"Did she sink?"

"Yes, but with none of the same fanfare or drama as the *Titanic*," I replied. Sarcasm was my go-to defense mechanism for emotional pain, and I was a master at it.

"Do you remember your coordinates?"

"They're in my log book, which went down with or burned up with her, whichever came first." I'd had that same logbook since I started sailing. It was thick, with my initials embossed on a worn leather cover. Losing it was more painful than losing my boat. I could replace one, but not the other. I gave her what I thought was my location. "But I can't be sure. That might have been the day before."

"No telling how far you drifted before we found you. The currents are pretty strong out here."

"It doesn't matter," I said, resigned. "That's what insurance is for."

"Why were you out alone?" Bert asked tentatively. The last time she asked I took her head off.

"I needed to get away."

"Tough week?"

"You don't know the half of it."

"Tell me."

❖

Bert

Alissa stiffened. I'd gone too far. She was rested and relaxed, and I figured this was a good time to find out more about what had happened on her boat. It was also a way to keep my mind off the fact that I had my arms around a beautiful woman in my bed. Obviously I was wrong on one count. I changed the subject.

"Is advertising as cutthroat as it looks on TV?"

"Like *Mad Men*?"

I chuckled. "I can't quite picture you in heels and pearls," I said. Actually, I could, and my pulse started racing.

"I happen to look fabulous in heels and pearls," she said.

"I bet you do." I remembered how good she looked the day she rescued me in the store. "So is it?"

"Not really. Well, in the big firms, yes, but not in mine."

"Tell me about yours." I hoped that question didn't shut down the conversation. Talking like this, in this position, was almost as intimate as making love. Silly, I admit, but I am a card-carrying romantic. I'd never let anyone know that, especially my crew, but that's the way it is.

I listened as Alissa gave me the shorthand version of Alissa Cooper Advertising. The words she chose and her melodious and soothing voice telegraphed class and sophistication.

"And you love it."

"Absolutely. I don't think there's anything else I'd rather do, except maybe sail around the world."

"But you don't have a boat." I restated the obvious.

"I'll get one."

"Just like that?"

"Yep, just like that."

"Do you always get what you want?"

"If I did I wouldn't be here. No offense," she added.

"None taken."

"When will we reach the fishing spot?" Alissa asked, her turn to change the subject.

"If we keep our heading and speed throughout the night we should be at our coordinates in another few days."

"Then what?"

"Then we start looking for fish."

"Just like that?" She echoed my previous question.

"Yep, just like that."

"I guess that's why you're so good at it."

"How do you know I'm good at it?"

"Look at this boat," she said, waving her hand. "It's fabulous and well taken care of, at least what little I've seen. I don't know anything about commercial fishing, but I do know boats, and this one didn't come cheap."

"My grandfather used to say a fisherman's boat is his lifeline and one you take care of before you take care of yourself."

"I never thought about it like that. I definitely see his point."

We lay there in silence for several minutes, and then Alissa sat up. Her hair was a mess, but that just slept-in-my-bed bed-head was definitely sexy. She tucked some of it behind one ear.

"I've got to use the head," she said, a light flush of red drifting up her neck.

"You know the way," I said, not moving. She looked at me as if expecting me to get up so she could get out. I much more preferred the thought of her climbing over me.

As Alissa moved, my weight shifted, so I was now leaning into her. She stretched one leg over mine, straddling my hips. I placed my hands on her hips to steady her, and when her arm followed she was directly over me. I sucked in my breath as the reality surpassed anything I could have imagined.

Her hair framed her face, her breasts almost touching mine, and I could feel the heat of her body above me. Our eyes met, and when hers went to my lips I swore I stopped breathing. My body instantly reacted, and the flash in Alissa's eyes let me know she realized it. I didn't move, couldn't move as I waited for Alissa to decide what she was going to do. I wanted her to kiss me. Hell, I wanted her to do more than kiss me, but I'd told her she was safe here, and damn if that didn't mean with me too. A knock on the door broke the spell, and Alissa jumped off me and headed toward the head. From over her shoulder she said, "It's for you."

Knowing the moment had passed and I had work to do, I said, "Yes, what is it?" after Alissa closed the door. The lock I had never used clicked loudly into place.

CHAPTER THIRTEEN

Alissa

OMG! I almost kissed her! Kissed her? Hell, I wanted my hands and mouth all over her and hers all over me. If somebody hadn't knocked on the door when they had, I wouldn't be in here with a locked door separating us. There wouldn't be anything between us, and I mean nothing except a fine layer of sweat.

"Jesus, Alissa, get ahold of yourself," I said quietly to my reflection in the small mirror. God, I had that just-fucked look, and I'd only fantasized about it for probably less than a minute.

What was happening to me? I'd heard about people who'd been in life-or-death situations becoming hyper-aware of their surroundings, including an exaggerated sex drive. Sex is pro-creative, life-giving, a matter of survival, and survivors often couple at the oddest times. Was that what this was? I'd almost died and my senses were in overdrive. My common sense had certainly drowned with my boat. Holy crap, I needed to get it together. I wasn't a hormone-driven eighteen-year-old.

I refused to make an ass of myself or make another mistake because of my near-death experience. I have more control than that, I kept telling myself as I washed my face. I don't even like her. No, that wasn't fair. I did like her when we had coffee, but circumstances were different now. I was angry and trapped, and I hated it.

I stalled as long as I could, not wanting to go out and face Bert. I didn't know if I was more embarrassed or appalled by my actions. It was more than obvious what had gone on in those brief seconds. I'd probably had thoughts similar to the ones I'd read on Bert's face written all over my own. No doubt about it. If that knock hadn't come, it might have been Bert's turn for her boat to go up in flames. I gave myself one last look in the mirror, took a deep breath, squared my shoulders, and opened the door.

Bert was sitting in the chair at the desk slipping on her boots. Her jeans were so faded I couldn't be sure what their original color was, and her T-shirt was short-sleeved and dark green. She'd pulled a fitted ball cap so low on her head that when she turned to look at me I could barely see her eyes. I didn't know what to say. I'm not normally tongue-tied or shy after an intimate encounter, and what had just happened was definitely an intimate encounter. But for some reason I didn't know what to say. I was completely out of my element, especially after I'd been so mean and hateful toward her. So instead, what came out of my mouth was incredibly stupid. "Bathroom's all yours."

"Thanks," Bert replied as she stood up.

The cabin was so small she had to pass by me to reach the bathroom, and to my complete humiliation I quickly stepped back as she approached. Something dark passed over her face before she said, "I told you that you were safe here, Alissa. And I mean it. That includes me."

"I can take care of myself. I don't need your protection," I snapped.

Bert only said, "I left some clothes on the bed. You probably don't want to run around in that all day." She waved her hand toward me, indicating her T-shirt and what little else I was wearing. Then she stepped into the bathroom and closed the door.

I didn't have any idea how long she'd be in there and tried to decide if I'd have enough time to change clothes or wait until she left the cabin altogether. Before I could make my decision the door opened and Bert stepped out, her hair wet, drying her hands on a towel.

"Breakfast is at six. There's plenty."

I nodded, said something that I think resembled thanks, and watched her close the door behind her.

"Jesus Johnson, Alissa, what the fuck!" I said, waving my arms up and down like a bird trying to catch flight. What the hell was going on? This should have been a perfectly normal conversation. Well, as normal as it could be after I'd floated in the ocean for God knows how long and been rescued by a stunningly butch fisherman and her crew of rough and rowdy deckhands.

I quickly made the bed, pulled the T-shirt over my head, and folded it neatly under one of the pillows. I stepped back, my mind flashing on what it felt like to be in that small space in Bert's bed. Butterflies started competing for my attention with the throbbing sensation between my legs. I told myself to ignore them both, pulled on the clothes, laced up the boots Bert had left for me, and exited the cabin.

I wandered up and down a few corridors before the smell of bacon and fresh coffee led me in the right direction. As I approached the galley the sound of deep male laughter drifted down the hall. My earlier nervousness returned. I was on their boat, their turf, plucked from the ocean like a mackerel that a seagull swoops down and nabs out of the water. We hadn't talked much last night. What would they say to me? What would I say to them? They probably thought I was a stupid female for being out on the ocean alone. They probably thought all kinds of things about me. But something told me that none of them would come right out and say anything. They would keep their absurd, lewd, and lascivious thoughts to themselves, and that suited me just fine. My stomach growled, and suddenly I was ravenous. I walked the last few steps and entered the galley, my head high.

All the sound in the room stopped with the exception of the bacon sizzling on the gas-stove burner. Six pairs of eyes turned my way, one of them belonging to the woman with whom I had just spent the night. By the looks on all of their faces they knew it too.

The four men around the table continued their conversation, I assumed where they'd left off when I walked in. I caught snippets of Hook talking about his son's driving lesson and Lefty complaining about how he was going to afford the fairy-tale wedding his daughter was planning. Bert was leaning back in her chair, her breakfast plate containing only crumbs of her meal, holding her cup of coffee in both hands in her lap. She was looking at me intently, and I wasn't sure if she was concerned about my physical health, mental health, or my level of sexual frustration. The first two were on the mend, and the third, not so much. Her questioning gaze did nothing to erase or even mitigate that issue. I noticed a bruise forming over her right eye. Where had that come from?

The food was delicious, albeit more than a little overwhelming. I managed to get down a little less than half of what was on my plate and two cups of very strong, delicious coffee. When each of the men got up from the table he pushed in his chair, rinsed his plate in the left sink, and stacked it in the right. This group of swarthy deckhands was more than a little tame and refined, and I wondered if that was Bert's doing. Admittedly I had no idea what to expect when being on a boat like this. I'd seen movies, but that was just theater. I'd read books, most of them fiction. Shows like *Deadliest Catch* and *Tuna Wars* probably held some grain of truth and a whole pile of show biz.

These men were clean and some had beards, but for the most part they were the kind of men you'd see in the local shopping mall. And judging by their conversation around the breakfast table, that's where some of them went on their free time with their wives and kids. Actually they looked like they were more fun at a party than some of the people I'd met at gatherings I was obligated to attend.

Bert remained behind as everyone left. God, I wish she'd stop looking at me like that. It made me nervous.

"How are you feeling?" she asked after her eyes did a not-so-quick once-over of the parts of my body she could see above the table.

"Fine." My standard I'll-take-care-of-myself reply.

"You need to rest today, push the fluids and get your strength back."

"I said I'm fine."

"You're on my boat, therefore my responsibility."

"I'm nobody's responsibility," I said quickly.

Bert looked at me carefully, her eyes drifting over my face, then back up to meet mine as if determining if I was telling her the truth.

"Make yourself at home," she said, standing. "There's plenty of everything."

"But only a five-minute shower," I said, trying to ease a little of the tension.

"Six minutes." She corrected me before giving me another medicinal look from head to toe.

I sat alone in the galley and helped myself to another cup of coffee. I still felt a little chilled. I didn't know if it was actually a physical condition or a mental one. I looked around the room, and, like everything else I'd been able to see on the boat, everything was neat, tidy, and well kept. It would never appear in *Architectural Digest* and certainly not *American Yachtsman*, but this was a working boat. Everything had a place and everything had a function. This was their office. People on this boat didn't entertain friends, colleagues, or clients. These were hardworking men and a woman doing what they did best, doing their job with what I could tell, so far, a sense of extreme pride. What a relatively uncomplicated way to live. What you saw was what you got. However, in everyone's job and life are the good and the bad, the joy and the drama, and I'm sure this group wasn't any different.

I found Bert on the bridge. She wasn't expecting me and obviously didn't hear me approach, so I had the luxury of watching her unobserved for several minutes. She was on her feet, focused on what was going on out the front window and the one to her right. Her fingers were resting lightly on three large knobs jutting out from the top of the console in front of her. From what I could see, they appeared to be controlling some type of crane moving slowly across the bow, storm clouds building in the distance.

I watched her fingers control the levers as if she were playing a fine piano or strumming the strings on a priceless harp. My body heated when I envisioned what it would be like if those same fingers were playing me. A voice crackled over the speaker just above her head.

"Roger that," Bert said, calmly repeating the request and ensuring there was no confusion. She repeated the maneuver several more times before I stepped a little farther into the bridge.

"You make that look so easy."

Judging by the way Bert reacted, or more appropriately didn't react, she must have known I'd been watching her.

"Well, you know, what they say, practice, practice, practice."

"May I?" I indicated the seat to Bert's left.

"Sure."

"You don't mind?"

"Mind what?" Bert asked, eyeing me quickly before turning her attention back out the window.

"Me watching you?"

She chuckled once. "And I thought all this time you were watching my crew," she said, confirming that she had in fact known I was observing her before I said anything.

"Well, them too," I said. This time her eyes stayed on me a little longer.

"Your crew is…" I searched for the words to describe them without making me sound like a snob.

"They're what?" she prompted me.

"Surprising."

"Surprising? How so?"

"Well, they…um…seem to be very good at what they do."

"And you find that surprising?"

"No…never mind," I said, trying to stop this conversation from derailing.

"Spit it out, Alissa."

"They're just not what I expected."

"What did you expect?"

"I don't know. A bunch of stinky guys that belch and fart and scratch." So much for not derailing.

Obviously Bert thought that description was pretty funny because she laughed out loud for several moments. My heart skipped a few beats.

When she finally stopped she said, "Yeah, well, you should have seen them on their first day. I told them I didn't think their mother had raised them like that and she'd be ashamed if she saw them doing those things. She'd probably slap their hand or smack them on the side of the head. Just because we're hundreds of miles from land they don't have a license to be uncivilized. This is my boat, my home, their home, and I expect everyone to treat it with respect. I don't want to go into a room every day and have the room stink. That's why we have a shower."

"Do most ships?"

"What? Have showers?"

I nodded.

"Ones this size do. Anything smaller, probably not. Can you imagine—"

"I'd rather not." I didn't want to even begin to, and my nose began to twitch. "Have you ever had any women?" Bert stared at me, an odd expression on her face. Suddenly I realized that my question hadn't come out right. The heat of embarrassment crept up my neck.

"As a matter of fact, I have." Her voice was sultry and held more than a little confidence.

"I meant as crew members," I clarified with still more than a little heat in my cheeks.

"Of course you did. Did you mean something else?" she asked with fake innocence.

"No." But it was an interesting question. Did I have other motives?

"I have one woman on my crew, Sandra. She's on maternity leave right now."

I raised my eyebrows. "Maternity leave?"

"Yes, maternity leave. She and her partner Margaret adopted a little girl from India. She's sitting out this trip. I've had a few others, but they didn't pan out. The work was too hard, wasn't what they expected, pressure from home to find something else, that sort of thing. I'll hire anyone who's willing to work hard, do as they're told, and keep their nose clean."

"Just that simple?"

"Just that simple."

"What do you do in the off season?"

"You're looking at it," she said, spreading her arms wide. "Repairs, upgrades, stuff like that."

"Do you live here?" I asked, indicating her boat.

"No. I have a boat at the marina. Actually she's not far from where you rescued me from debtors' prison at the grocery store. Do you want to call your family?" Bert asked without taking her eyes off what was going on out the front window. "I have a ship-to-shore radio."

"What time is it?" I really didn't know for sure. My sense of time was still out of whack, and I didn't even know exactly how much time had passed since breakfast.

"A little after seven," Bert replied after glancing at a clock above her head.

"My assistant isn't in yet," I said. "She usually gets in around nine."

"Won't your parents be worried?"

"My parents are somewhere in the Greek islands with my sisters."

"So the only person you want to call is your assistant?" Bert asked. That was a loaded question if I ever heard one.

"Yep, that's it." I didn't add anything more.

After a long silence, Bert nodded a few times. "Nobody special?"

I studied Bert's profile in the light streaming in from the windows. She had a nice, well-proportioned face and a small scar just below her left eye. Her hair flipped over her collar in the back. I'd thought she was attractive in the store, over our cup of coffee, and even now as she studied the compass to her left.

"If there were I wouldn't have agreed to let you buy me a coffee the other day. I don't cheat."

"It was just a cup of coffee."

"I don't believe that and neither do you," I said a little too adamantly. She missed my look of complete skepticism.

"A girl can hope, you know," Bert said. "Not the cheating part," she added quickly.

My heart skipped a little at a wild thought of where our coffee date might have gone from there. I wasn't opposed to having sex on the first date. Sex was sex, plain and simple. Nothing everlasting about it. That was my new mantra post-Ariel.

"Do you tell anyone when you go out?" Bert asked, returning her focus to her crew.

"How many times are you going to ask me that? I've already told you I do," I replied, trying not to bite Bert's head off. "I filed the required notice at the harbormaster's office. They don't expect me back until Sunday evening."

"Do you at least contact someone every day to check in?"

"No," I said. "I've been sailing for twenty-five years, and I know what I'm doing." I tried not to sound defensive, but the tone of Bert's questions was pushing my frayed buttons.

"Then that makes you…"

"Thirty-seven," I answered, even though it was none of her business.

"You'd think that being thirty-seven and after sailing for twenty-five years, you'd know better."

"What does that mean?" I snapped.

"Anything can happen out here," she said, waving her arm toward the vast ocean. "You could break down, have an accident, slip and knock your head on the boom. Or your boat could catch fire in the middle of the night, leaving you with a life vest and nothing else," she added, during the last part looking at me like *duh*.

"And you could hit a hidden iceberg," I shot back lamely. Why did I let her get to me like this?

❖

"Alissa." Bert's voice was warm and soft. I must have dozed off, because when I opened my eyes I was still sitting in the chair on the bridge and she was standing in front of me. *Shit, how had that happened?* The last thing I remembered was seething after Bert implied I was incompetent.

"Why don't you go lie down for a while?"

I was a little groggy so I must have been doing more than dozing. I rubbed my chapped hands over my face and grimaced. Shit, I'd forgotten about my sunburn. How could I do that? Every time I saw my reflection in a mirror I was reminded of a cooked lobster.

"Obviously I just took a nap," I said inanely. Having Bert this close and looking at me this intently turned my mind to mush. And watching her smile like she was doing right now left me a little rattled. "I'll make that call now," I said, pulling myself together.

Bert dialed in the ship-to-shore radio and handed it to me. I gave the operator the number to my office, and it was picked up on the second ring.

"Alissa Cooper's office," Marie answered, sounding professional.

"Hi, Marie, it's me."

"Alissa? My God. It sounds like you're a thousand miles away."

"Close enough," I replied. Crap. I really didn't know where in the hell we were. "Something's come up and I won't be in the office on Monday like I planned."

"Okay," Maria answered, sounding perplexed.

I looked at Bert, who nodded. Because the ship-to-shore call was really radio to phone, Bert was privy to our entire conversation.

"Alissa?"

"I'm here," I said, frowning. "I ran into a bit of trouble when I was out on the boat.

"OMG, Alissa, are you all right?" The panic in Marie's voice was clear. Though she was only twenty-four, she was like a mother hen.

"I'm fine, but my boat sank."

"What? Like the *Titanic*?"

"No, not like the *Titanic*." I shook my head. At times Maria acted like she was exactly twenty-four. "But I won't be in for a few weeks."

"A few weeks?" she shrieked. "How are you fine if you won't be in for a few weeks?"

"It's a long story, but a fishing boat on their way out on a six-week job picked me up. There are storms all around us, and since I'm not hurt, the coast guard won't come and get me, and the boat can't turn around and take me home. So I'll be in when the boat comes in."

"A fishing boat? With fisher*men*?" Maria was a city girl, and she'd find the idea of anything to do with fish that wasn't sushi appalling.

I cringed at her tone and what her few words implied. "It's not like that, Maria. The captain and her crew are fine, trustworthy people."

"*Her* crew?"

"Yes, *her* crew." I used the tone that always ended the conversation. "I need you to reschedule everything on my calendar until I get back." I proceeded to give all of my staff additional assignments, certain they could handle them. "Would you call my parents? They're somewhere in the Greek islands. Their itinerary is on my desk. You can leave a message at the hotel where they're staying. And call Rachel. If she finds out about this from someone else, I'll never hear the end of it." *I'll never hear the end of it anyway*, I thought. "One other thing. Get the billing information for a ship-to-shore radio call registered to the boat the *Dream* out of Boston. Put this call on my account and every other call I make from here."

Bert's head turned quickly to look at me. *No*, she said, mouthing the words.

I waved off her objection.

"Got it," she said, and I could hear her tapping the screen on her iPad. She never went anywhere without it. "And you're sure you're all right?"

I couldn't help but glance at Bert, who thankfully wasn't looking at me. I had no idea how to answer that question, so after a few more last-minute details, I ended the call and handed the handset back to Bert.

"You don't have to do that," Bert said, the muscles of her jaw working.

"I'm not going to argue with you about this. Ship-to-shore costs a fortune, and it was my call, so I'm paying." I had little control over my life these days, but I could have control over this situation.

"You're pretty good at issuing orders."

"Comes with being the boss. You know how it is," I added, especially after seeing her with her crew today.

Bert nodded. "Yes, I do, and with it comes the thrill of victory…"

"And the agony of defeat." The phrase had come from the introduction to the old ABC sports show called *Wide World of Sports*, the voice overlay of a downhill skier crashing down the mountain. Bert's laugh made me suddenly feel warm all over. I was glad she wasn't looking at me because my face was probably flushed as well.

"You took the words right out of my mouth," she commented.

The image of Bert's mouth, better yet, something of mine in Bert's mouth, overheated parts of my body farther south, and I squirmed.

"Come on." Bert took my elbow lightly, then lifted me out of the chair and toward the door. "I'll walk you back."

"I can find my way."

"Too bad. We're taking a break," she said, dropping her hand to the small of my back to propel me out the door and down the five steps.

I opened my mouth to refuse.

"Shut up."

I felt Bert's eyes on me as we maneuvered the narrow halls and descended another set of stairs. When we got to the door to her cabin Bert reached around me to open the door. The area was small and Bert's breast grazed my arm. I'm not sure, but I thought she froze for a split second before opening the door. My heart was pounding so loud she had to have heard it echo off the metal walls surrounding us. I hissed as my nipples hardened.

Bert jumped back. "I'm sorry. Did I hurt you?" she asked, looking at me from head to toe and lingering on my nipples obvious through the T-shirt.

"No, of course not," I lied. "Just a twinge under my arm."

She opened the door farther and I stepped inside. If I didn't know any better, I would have thought she pushed me inside. She didn't follow.

CHAPTER FOURTEEN

Alissa

The gentle rocking of the waves was a familiar friend versus a potential enemy, and I napped off and on that afternoon. Maybe it was because it was overcast, or maybe because I was in a familiar, safe place. I really didn't care why. I just knew I was finally starting to feel halfway decent as I followed my nose to the galley.

The table was set, and Lefty seemed completely at home in front of the stove as he stirred the contents of one pot while opening the oven door with the other hand.

"Can I help?" I asked, more out of politeness than anything else. I hoped he'd say no because I didn't know my way around a kitchen other than to grab a beer from the fridge and dump the last few Lucky Charms down the drain.

"Push that," he said, pointing to a button on the wall to my left.

I did as I was told and the button lit up under my finger. Nothing else happened. I looked at him for affirmation that I had done it correctly.

"The dinner bell," Lefty said, pouring the contents of the pot into a large plastic serving bowl. He pushed the rolls fresh out of the oven off the cookie sheet, and they tumbled over each other into a basket lined with a pristine white cloth. He covered them and handed me the basket. I was smart enough to know what to do with it.

"Grab a serving spoon from that drawer." He pointed to the one next to my right hip. "It goes in here," he said as he set the bowl in the center of the table. He started cutting thick slices of meat on a large platter, arranging them neatly.

The sound of footsteps pounding down the stairs behind me signaled the crew had arrived. One by one they filed in wearing clean shirts and smelling like Lava soap.

"You look rested," Bert commented, passing me the basket of rolls.

Several eyes checked me out, and then just as quickly, the men returned to dishing up their plates.

"I'll live," I replied honestly. "I should be ready to help in a few days." This time every eye was on me, and several forks of food stopped midway to open mouths.

"What?" I said, glancing around for some sign of what I'd obviously just stepped into, so to speak. "You don't expect me to sit here and do nothing for the next month," I said, more calm than I felt. If I had to, I'd go bonkers and maybe jump overboard again.

"I wouldn't put it that way," Bert said carefully.

"How would you put it?" My defensiveness started to build.

"Everyone on the *Dream* has a job and is fully trained in that position. We work well together, to the point that we know what everyone else is going to do before they do it."

"And?" I asked confidently.

"This is extremely hard work, not to mention dangerous," she added.

"Have you forgotten I was on a thirty-nine-foot double-mast sailboat?"

Bert looked at me silently, but I could hear the words in her head: "And look where that got you."

"I'm not a stranger to hard work."

"This is physical—"

"I can bench press two-oh-five, curl seventy, and leg-press three hundred pounds. My grip is strong, and I don't hurl my breakfast in a large swell." My voice was firm with conviction. No way was I going to let Bert think I was a lightweight. The crew had continued eating but were obviously waiting for Bert's return volley.

"I can't have a greenhorn on deck. It's too dangerous."

"Hook, did you learn on the *Dream*?"

"No, ma'am," he answered.

"Flick?"

"No."

I asked each man in turn, and my heart sank as each replied the same way. Until Limpet.

"Yes, ma'am. Captain Bert gave me a chance, and I promised to never let her down."

I raised my eyebrows and looked at Bert. "What's your next argument? You said it yourself. You've had women on the crew before. I'm different. I can do it."

Bert looked at me, and I wished I could read her mind. She glanced down at the table, and I cut her off before she went down the path I saw her headed.

"Don't even think about making me chief cook and bottle washer. If I don't kill your crew from food poisoning, they'll mutiny before the second day. I don't cook," I said, and saw Lefty stifle a grin from across the table. The men kept eating, but it was clear they were waiting for Bert's answer. "I've been on the water most of my life. I know what I'm doing."

"Not with this, you don't."

I didn't say anything, preferring to wait her out. I sat back and looked at her, my toughest I-can-do-this look on my face.

"Don't make me regret this," Bert said, her face grim. "You'll do exactly what you're told, exactly when you're told. No questions, no hesitation. You'll wear a lifejacket at all times on deck, and you won't go near the nets."

My heart skipped and jumped like it did when I was a little girl and got to go on a new adventure. I tried to remain serious, but a smile forced its way onto my face.

"Thank you," I replied sincerely. "You won't be sorry."

"I'd better not be," she said. "Okay, this conversation is over. You can all stop pretending you're not listening." Bert shook her head, but a smile peeked out of her stern face.

Conversation picked up, and it reminded me of one of the dinner scenes in a Tyler Perry movie. Several different conversations were going at once, and even though I'd known these people for less than three days, surprisingly I felt completely at home.

CHAPTER FIFTEEN

Bert

What in the hell was I thinking? Alissa no more belonged on the deck of the *Dream* than I did making a pitch to her top client. This was the last catch of the season, and if we didn't do well, the year would be a bust. Our previous trips hadn't netted more than a minimal catch, and with the cost of gas, maintenance, and payroll, I'd barely broken even. I didn't have time to keep an eye on Alissa, and I certainly didn't have anyone else to teach her. I could give her to Rock, but he had his own job to do. Same with the other guys. So I guess by default or design, Alissa was mine.

I passed the bowl of mashed potatoes, and our fingers touched when she took it from me. A jolt of electricity shot up my arm, took a sharp left, and headed south, stopping between my legs. I forced myself not to look at her but to focus on the conversation to my right. Hook was saying something about the nets when Alissa laughed. The electricity between my legs amped up, and this time I had to force myself not to moan. I shifted in my chair, which didn't help at all. Shit, it was going to be a long night. I realized that conversation around me had stopped and everyone was looking at me. Obviously someone had asked me a question.

"What?" I asked, feeling like an idiot.

"Is the *Dream* going into dry dock?" Hook asked.

"Yes, she's due a complete overhaul." I hoped my answer sounded like I knew what I was talking about. I did, but when I looked at Alissa, the throbbing in my crotch pushed out any remaining coherent thoughts in my head.

"What does that entail?" Alissa asked.

Thankfully Rock jumped in and answered the question, drawing her penetrating eyes away from mine.

I finished my dinner, relieved that no other questions were directed my way. Alissa held everyone's attention, including mine, as she asked and answered questions. I couldn't help glancing over at her more than a dozen times, enthralled when her face lit up as she talked about sailing, her voice becoming animated when she told a funny story. I knew I was in serious trouble when I realized the way she held her fork fascinated me.

I left the table as soon as possible, using the excuse of going to the bridge. No one seemed to notice. I sent Rock to the galley, checked the status of the gauges on the dash, adjusted a few knobs, and settled back in my chair. There was a half moon tonight, and the stars twinkled against the clear, dark sky.

I took a few deep breaths and a familiar calmness floated over me. This is where I was meant to be. This is where I called home. Sure, I had a place I referred to as home, which was really just a technicality. This place, this spot, this view, this peaceful, calm, almost serene feeling…I often thought that when I died I wanted to be right here. I've never been able to find the words to adequately describe just how right this place is. The phrase *mere words can't describe how I feel* was corny but one hundred percent true.

"You look like you were made for this."

I was so deep in my introspection that Alissa's voice startled me.

"Mind if I join you?" she asked from the doorway.

My crew knew this was my sacred time. They knew not to disturb me unless it was an emergency.

"No, come on in," I said, surprising myself.

"You looked deep in thought." Alissa stepped through the doorway. The bridge that could easily hold five or six people suddenly felt very small and intimate.

"Just relaxing," I said, which, although not the exact truth, was close enough.

"You love what you do," Alissa said, as much a statement as a question.

"Absolutely. I can't think of anything else I'd rather be doing."

"Have you always caught tuna?"

"Yes."

"How do you catch them?"

"It's pretty straight forward. We're part of a two-boat team. We locate the tuna, corral them into the nets, and then pass them into the transport pens."

"How do you find them?"

"We use a combination of sonar," I pointed to a black screen in front of me, "and the crow's nest," I pointed above my head, "to locate them."

"The crow's nest?"

"It's up top, thirty-eight feet above the bridge. When we get close to where we think the fish are, we man the nest."

Alissa looked confused so I added, "Tuna don't have the same type of gills as other fish, so they have to surface more often to warm up and digest their food. They eat constantly because they're so active. If it's calm you can see them break the surface or spot dark patches in the water."

"How do you get them into the net?" I asked, trying to figure it all out.

"We drop our nets," she pointed to the rear of the boat, "off the stern and slowly circle them, all the while baiting them to keep them interested and in one place. We close the net and voila," she opened both hands palms up, "a catch."

"How do you know what exactly you caught? Couldn't there be other things inside the net?"

"Flick goes into the water and takes a look at the size and quality of the fish, then reports back to me. We either keep them or…"

"Throw them back."

Bert laughed. "Actually we let them swim but the concept is the same."

"Then you haul them back to shore?" That sounded like an incredible journey.

"No, the holding pens are close by, and we tow the fish to the pens. We transfer them from our catch nets to the stronger, heavy-duty holding nets. They tow them back to the farm."

"The farm?"

"Because we're limited as to how much we can catch, we take what we trap, transfer them to the farm, and fatten them up. My brother runs the farm. It's been in the family for decades. My other brother, Steve, is the captain of the transport boat."

It was my turn to laugh. "How many brothers do you have?"

"Three."

"Any sisters?"

"Nope."

"What does your other brother do? No, wait," I said, holding up my hands to stave off her reply. "Let me guess. He runs the cannery. No, wait," I repeated. "He does something completely different. He's a doctor or a lawyer," I said, teasing her.

"Actually he's dead." Bert said evenly.

Oh, shit.

"He was in the army and was killed four years ago when his Humvee rolled over a land mine."

"Oh my God, Bert. I'm so sorry. I didn't mean…"

"It's all right. You didn't know. As a matter of fact, Mitch was a translator and obviously a lot smarter than the rest of us. But look where that got him," she murmured softly.

I didn't know what to say. I'd already stuck my foot, ankle, knee, and entire leg into that one and had no way to pull it out. Thankfully Bert threw me a lifeline.

"So that's how we fish."

"I can't wait to see it. When will you start?"

"Not for another few days. Over the years we've had to go farther and farther out for a catch."

"Over-fishing problem?"

"It was. It still is in some cases. About fifteen years ago the feds started instituting catch limits, which have helped. Didn't make the local fishermen happy, but if they'd kept on like they had been, there wouldn't be any fish left. Then where would we be?"

I tried unsuccessfully to hide a yawn.

"You should go to bed," Bert said. "I should have said it earlier. You're still recovering and need your rest."

"Are you coming?"

"Uh…" she mumbled.

"Don't tell me we're going to have this discussion about where you're going to sleep again." I crossed my arms over my chest. "Unless you don't want to sleep with me."

"Uh…" Bert stammered again.

"That's not what I meant. I mean, that's exactly what I meant but didn't mean it that way." Why did she make me say such stupid things?

Bert was flustered and I started to relax. "Well, now that you ask," she paused and turned to look at me, "I've thought of little other than that all day."

I'm sure my face flushed.

"I didn't look forward to sleeping in a chair or in the galley," she said, clearing up her statement.

"How long will you be?" I asked.

"Not long." She was fiddling with a knob on the dash in front of her. "Why don't you go on down? I'll be along in a few minutes."

I must be going out of my mind because I read very nasty things into almost everything she did and said. I'd rather she fiddled with my knobs, and the idea of going down was making my pulse pound in rather sensitive places. I had to get out of there before I either combusted or straddled her legs and fucked her right there in the captain's chair.

CHAPTER SIXTEEN

Bert

I almost slid out of my chair when Alissa asked me if I wanted to sleep with her. I was pretty sure I looked normal on the outside. Inside, however, was a completely different story. My heart started beating so hard I thought it would jump out of my chest and flop around on the floor. My pulse was racing like a car around the track of the Indianapolis Motor Speedway, and I would swear I stopped breathing.

YES, YES, YES, I wanted to say. *From the very first moment you smiled at me. Every time you look at me and when I look at you. When you laugh, when you have that look of concentration on your face when you're learning something new. When you were in my arms in the dark and first thing this morning.* God, I was turning into a sap.

What I said instead was something stupid and safe. I didn't want to be rejected, and I certainly didn't want Alissa to think she was required to sleep with me or that she owed me for saving her life. Lots of people would have played that card, but my honor got me nothing but a huge dose of frustration.

Rock came in to relieve me and I headed down to my cabin, butterflies dancing around in my stomach like a flash mob. I dawdled on my way down the stairs, and by the time I reached my cabin I was a nervous wreck.

"Jesus, Bert, it's not like you're planning to have sex for the first time," I said out loud in the empty hall. "No, it's worse. You want to have sex and shouldn't."

I knocked lightly on the door a few times before opening it several inches. "Are you decent?" *Are you decent? For God's sake, Bert. Keep your mouth shut.*

Alissa laughed. "I don't know if I'm decent, but you can come in."

I couldn't catch a break tonight. It wouldn't matter to me if Alissa was covered from ankle to wrist in a gunnysack or if she were wearing a red bra and matching panties. I would still want her. My hands shook as I stepped inside and closed the door behind me.

I dared a look and saw Alissa sitting up in bed, the covers pulled up to her waist. The scene reminded me of the one in the classic lesbian movie *Desert Hearts*, where Kay is in Vivian's bed waiting for her. Except in that movie she was naked, and here Alissa was wearing my T-shirt. Again, one scene wasn't sexier than the other. I exhaled and grabbed a clean T-shirt and boxers and headed for the shower.

"Six minutes," Alissa said, teasing me. "I saved you some hot water."

I needed much more than six minutes and definitely no hot water.

I did what I needed to in the shower and debated whether I should take care of business before getting into bed with Alissa. I'm not a one-and-done type of girl, and with my luck that would only make things worse. I stared at myself in the small mirror.

"You can do this. You're a grown woman, not a teenage boy," I said to myself, making sure my lips didn't move and Alissa heard what I said. But that was part of the problem. I was a grown woman and knew what I wanted and how it felt, and it had been a long time since I felt anything other than my own hand.

"You okay in there?" Alissa said from the other side of the door. *Great, now I'm even more shook up.* I opened the door before she came after me.

"Yep, just finishing up," I said, turning off the overhead light. The lamp next to the bed cast an intimate glow in the small room. When I was here alone, it provided just enough light to see, certainly not an intimate glow.

Alissa slid closer to the wall and lifted the covers. My throat closed at the obvious invitation, innocent as it was. When a woman lifts the covers, I interpret her action as a flashing sign that says *I want you to touch me and I want to touch you.* I broke out in a sweat. I had to get into bed, not stand there like a dazed virgin. God, why did everything I said or thought have to do with sex?

"Thanks," I murmured as I slid in. I tried to keep as much space between us as I could, but it was next to impossible in the small bed.

"Everything okay?" Alissa placed the covers over me.

"Of course," I lied.

"You seem a little…I don't know, nervous, or something."

"No, I'm fine," I lied again. "Just a little tired." I wondered how close to Hell I was going to go for lying three times in a row.

"You sure?"

"Yeah." What was one step closer, I wondered. Alissa turned on her side, facing me. Before she had a chance to say anything I asked, "So tell me something about Alissa Cooper I don't know." My mouth went dry when she smiled at me.

"Considering we haven't known each other very long, that's quite a list."

"Start anywhere."

"I thought you were tired," she said, drawing her eyebrows together. God, she looked cute doing that.

"It'll be like reading a book."

"Are you saying I'm boring?" she asked.

"No, no, not at all," I stammered. Jesus, what an ass, I thought.

"Relax. I'm just teasing you," she said, grinning. She tapped my arm, signaling me to lift it, and snuggled against my side.

I wish I could.

"I built my own house."

"You built a house?" I still wasn't sure if she was telling me the truth or pulling my leg. I decided to play along for something to get my mind off the fact that she was lying in my arms, her hair smelling like my shampoo.

"Actually, it was more of a remodel. But it was everything from shoring up the foundation to putting on a new roof," Alissa said, a hint of a smile on her face.

"How did you get started with that?" My body was still humming, but this conversation interested me.

"I bought the place after I got my first job. It was a dump but had lots of potential and in a neighborhood I loved. I worked with an architect on the design, and the rest was sweat, calluses, a broken nail or two, and lots of hard work."

"Wow" was all I was capable of saying. "I had no idea."

"Why would you? You don't even know me."

"I guess I never would have expected it from you."

"Why not?"

"Because you don't look like a handywoman."

"What does a handywoman look like?"

"She doesn't wear a business suit and shoes that probably cost more than I make in a month. Jesus, I bet you paid more for your watch than I make in a year."

"Is that a problem?" Alissa asked, stiffening in my arms.

"No, of course not," I said quickly. "At least not to me. I thought you were beautiful. You just didn't look like you would get your hands dirty and break a nail building a house."

Alissa relaxed. "Well, I do and I did. Several, as a matter of fact. And I almost broke my neck when I fell off a ladder."

"You fell off a ladder?"

"Actually, I fell off the roof. I was stepping onto the ladder when my foot slipped, and down I went."

"Jesus, Alissa, you could have killed yourself." This time my heart was racing at the thought of Alissa lying hurt on the ground.

"I was lucky, that's for sure."

Neither one of us said anything for quite some time. I didn't know what Alissa was thinking, but I knew she wasn't asleep. In a very short period of time I'd come to know the signs. The way her body slowly started to relax, muscle by muscle, and the way her breathing became deep and even told me she had fallen asleep.

I wanted to say something, anything, just to hear her voice. There was a cadence, a rhythm to the way she talked, her choice of words, a slight accent that came through on only a few words. But I didn't want to ruin the moment. With Alissa next to me in the silent night I felt a sense of calm I'd never experienced. I'd started to drift off when Alissa shifted, slightly snuggling closer to me.

"And a certain amount of mystery keeps a girl interested," she said sleepily.

My heart flipped and I was once again wide-awake.

CHAPTER SEVENTEEN

Bert

Her touch was feather-light but heated my skin nonetheless. It all started when Alissa straightened my T-shirt where it was all bunched up from sleeping. I lay on my back, Alissa curled against me. She pulled down on the hem, then smoothed out the wrinkles by running her hand across the fabric covering my stomach several times. I know I didn't have that many wrinkles, but when her fourth or fifth pass grazed the underside of my breasts, I didn't care.

I held my breath and prayed that her fingers would find their way under my shirt, then stifled a moan when they did. I didn't know if I should pretend to still be asleep or become an active participant. I chose the former, not wanting to risk her stopping what she was doing. If she thought I was asleep maybe she'd keep going or, if I was really lucky, go even farther. I kept my eyes closed and enjoyed the feel of her fingers on my skin.

Her hand grew bolder, and her touch turned from exploratory to caressing. Her path didn't quite reach my nipple, and she slipped one, then two fingers under the waistband of my boxers. I was so focused on my nipples screaming for attention that I couldn't help but suck in a breath when she did that. My back arched in a weak attempt to maintain contact when she slid them out. I felt her smile against my chest and had no doubt that she could hear and feel my heart pounding rapidly. When her palm grazed my nipple I moaned. There was no way she couldn't know I was awake. I couldn't do much in this position, but I caressed the places on her shoulder and arm that I could reach. Her skin was soft and warm, and I wanted to touch every inch. Even though I swallowed another moan when her fingers tweaked my nipple, my body immediately responded, leaving no doubt of how good that felt. She shifted up on an elbow, and at that point I opened my eyes.

Her eyes were crystal clear and the deepest shade of blue I'd ever seen. I detected darker flecks of color that I hadn't noticed before. But then again I'd never been two inches from them. She searched my eyes as if looking for a sign, a signal that she could kiss me, touch me, taste me. I was afraid of what I'd say if I tried to talk so I conveyed the *yes, please* that was screaming to get out through my own eyes. Thank God she was a mind reader.

Her kisses were soft. First one, then another, then another as she caressed my face with her lips. I lifted my chin, granting her access to my jaw, the curve of my neck, the contours of my collarbones. Her lips weren't the only thing exploring my body. Her hands roamed over my arms, my back, and slid under my shirt again. Her mouth returned to mine, this time hot and hungry for more. I buried my hands in her hair and pulled her close, deepening the kiss. She moved on top of me, her weight like a soft, warm blanket. She slid one leg between mine and pressed against me. Her mouth stifled my moan, but my body arched at the sensation.

My hands slid up and down her back and up again, taking the hem of her shirt with me. Our mouths separated for the instant it took to pull the impeding fabric over her head. Her mouth came back to mine, and she kissed me again as I had never been kissed before. Her mouth worshipped mine and I could have kissed her forever. Alissa, however, had other ideas.

She pulled away from me slightly and tugged my shirt over my head, then tossed it somewhere on the floor. She lowered herself again and closed her eyes as our breasts touched. I inhaled sharply at the sensation, and my heart pounded.

Alissa returned to my lips and kissed me long and deep. I felt her hands at the waistband of my boxers again. I mimicked her moves, and this time it was her turn to moan. She slid her hand inside, and I held my breath for the instant she touched me.

There would never be another time like this. The first touch, the first evidence of slick wetness on fingers. She pulled her mouth away from mine and dropped her mouth to my breast as her fingers traced the outline of my sex. I lifted one leg, giving her more access, and didn't try to temper my moan of desire.

"Bert?"

I heard my name in the distance, coming toward me like sound in a fog.

"Bert, wake up."

This time the sound was louder, and even through my sex-crazed brain the words weren't what I was expecting to hear. I opened my eyes and looked into the darkness. Alissa wasn't above me; she wasn't even on top of me. Two seconds later I knew I still wore the clothes I'd gone to sleep in. What the hell?

"Bert. Wake up."

I lifted my head and looked around. Alissa was sitting up beside me. It was still dark, but the porthole beside the bed let in enough light to let me see a look of concern on her face.

"You were dreaming. You were moving around and moaning like you were in pain."

OMFG! Alissa wasn't making love to me. It was all a dream. I wanted to crawl between the seams in the tile on the floor and never come out again. I was completely humiliated. No, that wasn't a strong enough word. I was mortified.

"You're sweating," Alissa said, touching my forehead.

Without thinking I grabbed her hand and almost yanked it away. I was so keyed up from my wet dream I wasn't certain I wouldn't come instantly if she did touch me for real. Judging by the look on her face, I think I'd frightened her. I loosened my grip and rubbed her wrist.

"I'm fine. Sorry. You just startled me. That's all."

"You scared the shit out of me."

"Sorry," I said again, getting up. I needed distance from the memories of my wet dream starring Alissa. "I'm going back to check the bridge." It was a weak excuse but one that got me out of that very small room.

CHAPTER EIGHTEEN

Bert

What in the hell was I thinking when I'd agreed to let Alissa work the boat? Even more stupid was that I had assigned her to me. God, I needed my head examined. That meant I had to spend hours with her showing her everything on the boat, listening to her voice as she asked questions. I stood beside, behind, and in front of her, catching a whiff of the smell of my shampoo in her hair, touching her hand to show her the correct grip, holding her waist as she leaned forward to grasp the end of a net. She was a bright, attentive, very fast learner. Out of all the deckhands I've ever trained, I have to admit she'd picked up the necessary skills quickest and was definitely the best looking. Her skin had tanned into a healthy glow, and her strength returned a little every day. I found myself looking forward to our morning sessions.

One afternoon a storm materialized out of almost nowhere, a common occurrence in these waters. It was the third one since we picked her up and by far the most fierce. As the sky darkened, the crew, including Alissa, checked the gear and secured anything that wasn't fastened down. It wasn't long before the height and intensity of the waves increased to dangerous levels. The storm was directly in our path, and to go around it would result in delay and thousands of dollars in lost revenue.

The boat was getting more and more difficult to control in the high seas. She vibrated as her powerful engines struggled to push through the rough water. I stood on the bridge, my feet shoulder width apart, my hands tight on the wheel. The windows were closed and I was dry, but I had my life vest on over my sweatshirt. I wasn't taking any chances. I'd seen far too many rogue waves in this sea, and if I were unlucky enough to be swept off, I'd have at least half a chance to survive. The door to my left opened, admitting a blast of cold air, more than a few raindrops, and Alissa.

"What are you doing up here?"

"I came to see if you needed anything."

"You came to see if I needed anything?" I was incredulous. We were in the middle of a monster tropical storm, and she came up to see if I needed anything? What the hell did she think she was, a waitress? "Why aren't you below with the rest of the crew?" That was almost true. Hook was to my right, watching the radar for any break in the storm.

"I came to see if you needed anything," she repeated.

"Everyone else is in their bunks waiting for the storm to pass. And that's exactly where you should be." I was furious that she was risking her life by being up here with me and not tucked safe in my cabin.

"I'm not afraid of a little storm," Alissa replied defensively, nodding toward the rain blasting the windows with sheets of water. The boat lurched forward, and she grabbed the rail that was just below the dash with both hands. The rocking of the boat was becoming more severe.

"This is not a *little storm*," I snapped back, moving the wheel three quarters of a turn to the left. "Have you ever been in a storm with gale-force winds of," I looked at the wind-speed indicator, "seventy knots?" When she didn't answer I said, "I didn't think so." For some reason the *I told you so* didn't feel quite as satisfying as I'd thought it would.

"Fine. Then I'll go back below deck." She started to reach for the door.

"Stay here," I shouted. It was bad enough I was afraid that she was up here with me. It would be worse to imagine her going back out into the storm to head below.

For the next several hours the storm was relentless, giant waves of water splashing over the bow. My arms ached from fighting the wheel, but I refused both Alissa and Hook's offer to relieve me. This was my boat, my crew, and my responsibility.

Finally, after hours of being tossed around in the ocean like my nephew's plastic boat in the bathtub, a rainbow peeked through the clouds.

"Look!" Alissa said excitedly, pointing out the window. There was a break in the storm, and the patch of blue sky was a welcome sight. Her smile was infectious, and the muscles in my shoulders started to relax. I tilted my head from side to side to relieve some of the stress in my neck. I think I even started breathing again. I unbuckled my life vest and tossed it on the seat beside me.

Alissa moved behind me and started rubbing my neck. God, that felt good. No, it felt fucking fabulous. Her fingers were cool but her touch was warm, and the longer she touched me the more difficulty I had paying attention to what I was supposed to be doing. More than once I felt my eyelids close and my eyes begin to float to the back of my head before I forced myself awake. It would not be good for me to fall asleep at the wheel.

"Thanks," I said, shrugging my shoulders and stepping away from Alissa's magic hands. "I think it's safe enough now for you to go below. But keep your vest on until you get there," I added. I didn't look at Alissa, actually, but turned slightly away, effectively dismissing her from the bridge. She didn't say anything as she closed the door behind her.

I glanced at Hook, who was looking at me strangely. "Don't say it," I warned him. "I mean it, Hook," I said when he opened his mouth. Thankfully he closed it and went back to writing something in the ship's log beside him.

This time when the door opened it was Rock relieving me for a few much-needed hours of rest. I briefed him quickly but thoroughly and headed to my cabin.

CHAPTER NINETEEN

Alissa

It was three more days until we got to wherever Bert planned to fish. During that time I learned how to play hearts and pinochle and lost all of the five dollars Bert staked me in poker. Luckily it wasn't strip poker or I'd have lost a lot more.

On the afternoon of the thirteenth day at sea, the *Dream* slowed its engines and Bert turned on the sonar. Rock climbed up into the crow's nest with a water bottle and a pair of binoculars.

I was on deck next to Hook, my chaperone for the day. Earlier this morning I'd convinced Bert to let me help, and even though I knew she wasn't too happy about it, she agreed, with the stipulation that I covered myself from my head to my toes to protect my skin from the sun. As an extra layer of protection I slathered SPF45 sunscreen over my arms and hands. I was trying to rub it into my shoulders when Bert knocked on her cabin door.

"How did those fit?" she asked from the outside of the door. She had given me a pair of lightweight GoreTex pants and a long-sleeve shirt to wear.

I opened the door with one hand, holding a tube of sunscreen in the other. I had on the pants and only a thin, sleeveless T-shirt, and Bert gave me the once-over, lingering on my breasts before she looked at my face and, ultimately, my eyes. The tension and temperature in the room skyrocketed at the unmistakable heat and desire I saw in her eyes. We'd spent the last eight nights in the same bed, and I'd had at least half a dozen dreams about what would happen if she put her hands on me.

"Let me help you with that," Bert said, taking the bottle out of my hand. "Where do you need it?" I could swear her voice was a little shaky.

"My neck and shoulders," I answered, *my* voice also a member of the shaky club. I turned around, my throat suddenly very dry.

Warm, strong hands rubbed the lotion over my skin, starting at the back of my neck and moving across my shoulders. When her slick hands slid under the straps of the T-shirt to coat that area, I swear I felt waves crash around in my stomach. Her hands moved down my arms, slowly rubbing in more lotion. Then she stepped closer. Her breath on my neck sent chills down my spine and warmth in regions farther south.

God, her hands felt good on me. Night after night I'd dreamed of what this would feel like, and it was nothing compared to the real thing. And this was only medicinal. If Bert touched me for real, the top of my head would probably blow off, or maybe other parts would.

"I want you on the bridge with me today," she said, rubbing the lotion onto my arms.

"You already said I could help." I somehow managed to say from my very dry mouth.

"We're scouting for the school, and as soon as we find it, controlled chaos will break loose. I want you out of the way."

I turned around and faced Bert. "You've spent the last three days showing me what to do. I'm not going to sit up here twiddling my thumbs while the guys do all the work."

Bert studied me for several moments, obviously weighing the pros and cons of my request. Her situation was interesting because she was always so decisive about what needed to be done and by whom. She never hesitated when someone asked a question.

"All right," she said in a tone more resigned than accepting. "I'll put you with Hook today. You need to do exactly what he says—"

"When he says to do it, no questions asked." I could tell she was fighting a smile so I smiled for her. "I can follow directions, Bert. I won't get hurt. But if I do it's my own fault, and I promise not to sue you," I added, trying to get her to not look so serious. I didn't succeed, as she had her game face on this morning.

It was late afternoon when I finally had the chance to prove myself. "What should we be on the lookout for?" I asked Hook. We were standing next to the outer rail of the deck.

"If it's flat and calm, you'll see the fish break the surface. Tuna come to the surface to warm up and digest their food faster," Hook said when I stared at him, confused. "Up in the crow's nest," he turned and pointed above our heads, "you can see the patches of color of the schools. Come on. We've got to bait."

I helped Limpet and Hook lug boxes of frozen bait from the freezer below deck to the top deck. Hook passed around his pocketknife for each of us to use to open our boxes. When Limpet passed it to me he said, "Be careful with that. You can shave your legs with it and lose a finger." He was right, as the blade sliced through the thick tape like it was warm margarine. Lefty came up with a long pole with a net on the end, which he told me was for scooping out the fresh bait in the hold. I glanced over my shoulder and saw Bert through the window, concentrating on something in front of her.

"What do we do now?" I asked Hook after the boxes were open.

"When the captain gives us the go-ahead, we start baiting the water."

"Why fresh and frozen?"

"Tuna won't go after just frozen bait. Eventually it sinks to the bottom, so we throw in some live now and then to get and keep their attention."

I scoured the water, hoping to see whatever Bert and Rock were trying to find. Bert had told me it would be a large school of tuna, and I had seen several schools during various times I had taken my boat out.

I pulled one of Bert's spare hats down low on my forehead and adjusted the sunglasses she'd loaned me as well. The blast of an air horn startled me, and immediately after that Hook shouted, "Let's go."

He and Limpet started tossing fish from the boxes into the water. I watched for a few minutes to see if there was any special way to do it, then grabbed a handful and tossed. The fish were about two inches in circumference and about four to six inches long. It didn't take long for my hands to get really cold.

After only fifteen minutes of baiting, I had to switch sides and toss with my other hand. This and just about every other thing I'd done on the boat had told me I was spending way too much time behind a desk. I vowed to make it to the gym at least three times a week when I got home.

It didn't take long before sweat escaped from my hatband and slid down the side of my face. A drop or two dripped into my eyes before I could wipe it away and stung like a bitch. At least I'd somewhat recovered from my original sunburn, and my nipples were pretty much healed as well, thank God. I put on the magic balm Bert gave me that first day three times a day, and it worked. It smelled bad but I didn't care. It wasn't like anyone was going to get close to my nipples. Bert didn't seem interested. But I needed to concentrate on what I was doing, not stand there having wet dreams.

We spent the next few hours watching the surface of the water for any signs of the catch. My head was pounding and my eyes felt like they were being pulled out of their sockets, but I refused to give in. I couldn't. First of all I never quit, and second, and most important, I certainly couldn't after my speech to Bert in the galley the other night.

"Tuna!" Rock shouted from the crow's nest.

I looked up at him, shielding my eyes from the sun. He was pointing to the left of Hook and me, and I turned back to see what he was talking about.

"There," Hook said excitedly, pointing toward a faint splash in the water about a hundred yards out. "Do you see it?"

"I'm not sure what I'm looking for, but I think so," I admitted.

"Drop the net." Bert's voice over the loud speaker startled me.

The large crane that Bert had been maneuvering the other day started moving. Slowly a large net slid off the back of the boat and into the water. I heard the engines slow as Bert steered toward the school. The net had buoys at the top to keep it from sinking. Bert had explained that once the net is around the school, the men gradually winch in a steel draw cord running along the bottom of the net to close it. That way they force the tuna to swim in a small area.

The hum of the winch started and didn't stop for over an hour. Slowly it pulled the net in and secured the catch.

Hook turned to me. "Our job is done for now."

Flick, decked out in full diving gear, slid into the water. Once the tuna were in the net, his job was to go into the water and survey the trapped fish. If they weren't in the legal size range, they had to be released. Forty minutes later his head popped out of the water, followed by his raised arm, his thumb in the up position.

"What happens now?" I asked, thrilled to stop tossing fish into the sea. My arms were killing me.

"We transfer the tuna to the transport nets." Hook pointed to another ship off our starboard bow. "The transport nets can hold about ten thousand fish, and they're built to withstand storms and rough seas. Their net is made of high-density polyethylene tubing filled with polyurethane foam. It's the tubing normally used for sewer pipes or gas distribution where durability is critical."

That was interesting but way too much technical information for what I needed. "Then they haul the tuna back to the…what's it called? The farm?"

"Right. The fish are kept and fattened up in tuna farms. It's a lot cheaper to do it this way than try to find, catch, and transport full-grown fish."

"How much is a net full of fish worth?" I asked, curious and fascinated.

"One trip can bring home twenty tons of juvenile tuna worth twenty million."

"Dollars? Twenty million dollars?" I looked back at the net circling the school. The amount was incredible.

"Yep. But that's the cost of the tuna when they're harvested. We don't get twenty million for what's in that net."

"That's a relief," I said. "I'd hate to think we'd have to fight off pirates on the way home. How long does it take to get to the farm?"

"From here, about two weeks. We stay behind the transport ship in case we have a problem. I was on one ship, before the *Dream*, and the tow rope snapped. Three hundred feet of tow rope sank to the bottom of the ocean like that." He snapped his fingers. "Fish scattered everywhere. We never caught them all. It took another week to round up enough to bring back."

The rest of the day I watched as Bert and her crew expertly maneuvered the catch net in place adjacent to the transport nets. Several divers were in the water, Flick included, making sure everything was exactly where it should be. Before Hook left to help with the transfer, he explained that this was the most difficult part of the catch.

Our catch net had to be lined up exactly with the transfer net so that when we opened ours, the fish swam into the other net. If the nets weren't lined up precisely where they needed to be, a few fish might escape and the entire school would follow.

It was several hours later when Bert hoisted the giant net above the deck to its resting place against the boom. Since it was so close to dark, the crew secured it and everyone called it a day.

❖

Alissa

It was late in the afternoon of the fourth day scouting for catch. We had netted a school earlier in the morning but released them due to their size. I still felt Bert's eyes on me, but not all the time, as I had for the past few days. I'd proved to her that I could do as I was told: stay out of the way and not get hurt. We were baiting the water when Limpet asked innocently, "How did you know you liked girls?"

Hook slapped his arm. "Shut up, you dumb shit. You don't ask something like that. It's none of your business."

I smiled at Limpet, who was now blushing nine shades of red. "It's okay. I don't mind when someone asks questions. As a matter of fact, I prefer it. It's when they don't and draw assumptions and jump to wrong conclusions that pisses me off." Limpet turned to Hook with a smug look on his face.

"I guess I was about seventeen or eighteen. All my friends were all excited about their date to the senior prom, and all I could think about was how much I wanted to dance with Suzanne Alexander."

"Did you have a date?"

"Yes. Rand Martin was my date. He was a cowboy, complete with boots, hat, and a belt buckle the size of your palm." I chuckled, remembering the tall, skinny cowboy. "Every girl on campus wanted him to ask her, but for some reason he asked me."

"I'd ask you to the prom," Limpet said.

"And I'd go with you," I replied honestly. "I'd probably have more fun with you than I did with Rand." I tossed another handful of bait into the water.

"What happened? Didn't he dance?"

"No. Just the opposite. He was a great dancer and loved to dance. But he also had a hard time keeping his hands to himself.

I guess he'd heard all the rumors that everybody has sex on prom night, and he wasn't about to be left out. He had a hard time keeping that thought to himself, if you know what I mean," I said, raising my eyebrows. Both men snickered.

"Dang, I wish that was how it was at my prom," Hook added, joining the conversation. "I think the chaperones outnumbered the students two to one. I was lucky to get a good-night kiss."

Limpet and I laughed. "You're making up for it now," Limpet said with more than a little envy in his voice. "So did you ever get to dance with that girl?"

"No, but I did get to kiss her a few days later." I raised my eyebrows a few times like Groucho Marx, and Limpet and Hook both sat up straighter.

"Really?" Limpet asked excitedly.

"Yep, right on the lips." And it was better than I ever imagined.

"What did she do?" Hook asked.

"Kissed me back."

"No." Hook gasped. "Did you know she'd do that?"

"Not a clue," I said, remembering the feel of her soft lips on mine. "She tasted like cherry ChapStick and was a really good kisser." I didn't share the part where she slipped her tongue in my mouth.

"Wow. Then what happened?" Limpet asked.

"She slapped me." I could almost still feel the sting in my cheek.

"What?" they said simultaneously.

"Yep, right across the cheek." I laid my hand on my face where she slapped me. "She called me sick and disgusting and told me never to touch her again."

"But I thought you said she kissed you," Limpet said, asking for clarification.

"She did, and very enthusiastically I might add. I guess once she realized *who* she was kissing, she freaked." And boy did she ever. "She called me every ugly name in the book, then turned and ran. She made sure I saw her making out with her boyfriend after school. But she was really running from herself, not me."

"Whatever happened to her? Did she turn gay?"

Hook slapped Limpet again in the arm, this time more playfully. "What rock did you just come out from under? You don't *turn* gay."

Hook was more insightful that I'd given him credit for. "I have no idea. She went out of her way to avoid me the last two weeks of school, and I never saw her again."

"Jeez, and I thought my first kiss was awkward," Hook said ruefully.

"So are you seeing anyone now?" Limpet asked. "What?" he said, dodging Hook's third smack. "I'm just being polite and asking. It's not like I'm hitting on her or anything."

"It's okay," I replied, and realized it was. I usually didn't like to talk about myself, but with these guys it felt natural. "No. I'm not seeing anyone right now."

"That's surprising," Hook said. "I mean a good-looking woman like you. And I'm not hitting on you either," he added quickly. "Unless you want me to?" He was clearly joking.

"Thanks, Hook, but I'm afraid you're not my type." I winked at him.

"What is your type?"

"Yeah. What was your last girlfriend like?" they both asked in a chorus of questions while we tossed slimy, wiggling fish into the sea.

"A conniving bitch," I said without thinking.

"I had one of those," Hook said, nodding.

"Mine is serving four to ten in McDowell Prison in Massachusetts."

Both men froze mid-toss to look at me. Hook recovered first and threw his handful in the water, then reached into the box in front of him. "Shit, and I thought mine was a mean one."

"She wasn't mean, but she did embezzle one million, four hundred eighty-two thousand, one hundred forty-nine dollars from me. They tossed her ass in jail and I hope they lose the key." The venom in my voice was clear.

"Shit, Hook. Colette only stole your TV," Limpet noted.

I decided I should probably keep my mouth shut from now on, but something about these guys made it easy to talk to them. Maybe it was because after this we'd never see each other again. Or maybe because they were completely nonthreatening and nonjudgmental. It didn't really matter. My secret was out now.

Bert's voice came over the speakers just below the windows on the bridge. "Drop the net."

Chapter Twenty

Alissa

"Alissa, I'm so glad you finally called," Marie said. It had been only a few days, but that could be a lifetime if there was a problem.

"What is it, Marie?"

"A helicopter. A helicopter that will come and pick you up." She spoke so fast I could hardly understand what she said.

"A helicopter?" I asked, her statement not making sense.

"Let me back up," she said. "Remember a few years ago we did that work for Beckworth helicopter? Well," she said, not giving me the chance to say yes or no. "Mark called them a few days ago and told them what happened and where you are, and they said they'd send one of their helicopters to pick you up." Marie made her statement in one long sentence with no breath in between anything.

A helicopter? I was still trying to wrap my head around it. They would come and get me? I could be off this boat and sleeping on my own bed as early as tonight.

"He said if there's no place to land, they can pick you up in a basket or something like that. Mark asked that I put you through to him as soon as you called."

"Wait, Marie," I said hurriedly. "What do you have for me first?"

It was our third call, and she rattled off several things that I really didn't pay too much attention to. I guess I answered them appropriately because she didn't ask me any follow-up questions. I kept thinking about the helicopter and the real possibility—no, probability that I'd be off the boat tonight. I'd been here almost two weeks.

I quickly thought back to yesterday when we readied the boat for the catch. I'd helped Limpet and Rock check the nets, and we'd spent most of the day telling jokes and talking smack about women. All three of us agreed we couldn't live with them or without them. I liked these guys. I enjoyed their company and learned something from them every day. They were a different breed of men. They took pride in what they did, loved their job even though it took them away from their friends and family for weeks at a time, and respected Bert. Bert had said I had nothing to fear from these guys, and she was right. Never once had I caught them looking at me with anything other than curiosity or respect. Christ, Limpet, and Hook still called me ma'am. I worked hard and hadn't slept this well in—well, I can't remember how long. And then there was Bert.

Bert Coughlin was the most interesting woman I'd ever met. She was book smart, street-smart, and water smart. Last night at dinner she recited Shakespeare, and this morning she was in the engine room helping Rock fix an oil leak. She voiced her opinion on various topics we discussed but kept her politics to herself. She was strong and confident, a package that was just downright hot.

I tried not to think about Bert as hot, but that was getting more and more difficult. She often worked in just a pair of cargo shorts and a wife-beater T-shirt, her muscles defined under a glow of sweat. Her wrap-around Ray Bans protected her eyes from the sun and the harsh glare of the water. Her skin was tanned from the sun, callused from hard work yet soft to touch.

My fingers twitched on the radio handset to touch her again like I had last night.

I had awoken to find Bert sleeping soundly beside me. I couldn't resist the urge and the opportunity to slide my hand under her shirt and touch her skin.

I would have made a good SEAL or army ranger or whatever other special forces there were because I successfully completed my mission without being detected. Slowly, and I mean slowly, I moved my hand from where it was resting on top of Bert's shirt to under her shirt without being discovered. It seemed like my maneuver took forever, but when my fingertips touched her warm skin, I knew it was worth it. My heart was pounding out of fear I'd get caught and excitement for what I was doing. I had my head on Bert's chest, and the rhythmic beating of her heart and the steady cadence of her breathing confirmed she wasn't aware of my explorations.

Why was this happening? Just a few days ago I didn't even like her very much. I knew I probably shouldn't be doing what I was doing, but that didn't stop me. Many agonizing minutes later the complete palm of my hand was resting lightly on Bert's hard, flat stomach. She was warm, sending her warmth through my hand to other parts of my body. Without thinking, I pressed my body closer and she shifted, tightening her arms around me.

I froze, because when she moved my hand was now cupping her breast. Oh, Mary Mother of God, it fit perfectly in my hand. Her breast was warm and heavy, and when she exhaled, her nipple grazed the tip of my fingers. I was in agony because I wanted to do more but couldn't. My heart was pounding so hard I was surprised Bert hadn't woken. If the roles were reversed I certainly would be awake—wide-awake and more than ready to go. I decided to stop thinking and simply relax and enjoy the sensation of being in Bert's arms.

When I woke this morning Bert wasn't in bed, but the sheets were still warm, and I had a moment of panic. I had fallen asleep in that position, and had I still been there when Bert woke? She wasn't in the galley either, and we'd spoken only a few words before we made this call.

The sound of Mark's voice pulled my lustful thoughts back to the here and now.

"I'm sorry, say that again?" I asked, unable to keep my eyes from darting to Bert. She was looking at me with an expression I couldn't read.

"I said give me your longitude and latitude, whatever that is, and Ian Beckworth himself will fly out and pick you up. He said he'd bring his X15 Jet ranger. You know, the one we did the campaign for."

I did remember and I wanted to forget. The contract itself had been fun, challenging, and quite lucrative, but dealing with the grandson of the founder had been just the opposite. Young Beckworth was in his early twenties and full of himself, like most men his age. I had to walk a tightrope to not piss him off and lose the account by telling him to take his entitled dick and shove it up his tight ass. No way did I want to be indebted to Baby Beckworth, even if it meant spending the next several weeks on the *Dream*.

Bert was looking at me intently. "I don't know when we'll stop, Mark, and when we do, the helicopter will scare away the fish." I was making it up as I went, but Bert's nod of agreement told me I was right.

"But he can get you off that boat," Mark said in just about the same tone Maria had the first time we spoke. When did my crack crew turn into elitist snobs?

"Let me think about it," I said.

Bert's eyebrows shot up, and she glanced at me before turning her attention back out the window in front of her.

"What's there to think about?" Mark asked. I could see his confused face in my mind. It always gave away what he was thinking. He was probably pacing back and forth in front of his desk too.

"Mark, I've got to go," I lied. "The captain needs the radio. We'll talk in a few days." I gave the call sign letters and signed off.

Bert's eyes were on me when I reached above her and hung the radio handset on its clip. "I don't need the radio," she said.

"You will," I said, my thoughts jumping around from this entire conversation.

"You have a Beckworth X15 available to come and get you?" Bert whistled. "I never would have suspected you have those connections."

"I don't. My firm worked on a campaign for Beckworth a few years ago."

"Obviously you made quite an impression. That kind of help doesn't come cheap."

"Neither does working for Baby Beckworth," I said without thinking. Bert's eyebrows rose even farther. "He thought I was part of the services. Good-looking guy who probably had never been told no in his entire pampered life, especially by a woman."

"And that's why you didn't jump at the chance to get out of here?"

"I admit the offer's tempting."

"I hear a but in there."

"But I don't want to owe him anything. He'll expect me to pay up in one way or another."

"Does he know you're a lesbian?"

"Therein lies the challenge for him."

"Wow," Bert said, shaking her head. "Do you run into that often?"

"No, at least not in the last few years," post-Ariel, I thought. I'd often wondered how many of my clients Ariel had fucked as well as me. I shuddered.

"Are you okay?" Bert asked, a look of concern on her face. "Maybe you should take him up on it and get checked out. Make sure you're all right."

"No," I said firmly. "I'm fine. Just a bad memory slicing through my head." After several minutes of silence I got up the nerve to ask, "Do you want me to leave?"

Several more moments passed before Bert spoke. "This isn't your job. You have a life on shore. The coast guard called earlier. They can be here tomorrow."

That didn't answer the question and I told her so.

"It's up to you. We have enough food and water, so that's not an issue," she said, no closer to saying if she wanted me to stay or to go.

"Do you need an extra hand even if it belongs to a greenhorn?"

"I can always use one."

"Wouldn't you like to have your bed back?"

Finally she looked at me. "You haven't heard me complain, have you?"

"Would you? Complain, I mean?"

Bert was looking right at me, our eyes locked. Her gaze didn't waver and neither did mine.

"Yes."

"Then I'll stay," I said, just before dragging my eyes away from hers but not before I saw a flicker of desire in her eyes. My heart raced.

CHAPTER TWENTY-ONE

Bert

"Man overboard!"

I looked out the window, across the stern. Hook was waving frantically and shouting. I hit the large red button, and the winch deploying the net stopped, leaving half of it hanging from the boom, the other in the water. I killed the throttle on the ship's engines and threw the gear into neutral. I didn't want to put us into reverse until I knew who was in the water and where. It was bad enough they were in the water; they didn't need to get chewed up by the massive propellers. I ran out onto the deck behind the bridge.

Hook and Blow were leaning over the rail, and Limpet and Lefty were running toward the skiff that was secured on the port side. Rock was pointing at something from his perch up in the crow's nest. Where was Alissa? My heart beat faster. She was supposed to be with Hook today, and the last time I'd seen her she was tossing bait with him and Limpet. My eyes quickly scanned the deck. There was no sign of Alissa. I started to panic.

"It's Alissa," Limpet shouted before I had a chance to ask. He pointed to the water off the starboard side. I ran back inside the bridge, grabbed my binoculars, and ran back outside. I saw something off to my right, put the glasses up to my eyes, and started to search. The water was choppy today, making it difficult to keep my line of focus.

Wait…what was…there! There she is, I said to myself as I spotted Alissa. She was caught on one of the buoys that kept the top of the net above the water. Thanks to the life vest I insisted she wear, she too was on top of the water, but, depending on the whims of Mother Nature, that could change at any second. Thankfully we'd been moving at only five knots so *Dream* hadn't traveled far after I killed the engine, though she was still about a hundred yards away.

Flick was also on the bridge, and I scampered down the two flights of stairs to reach the rear deck. By the time I got there, Alissa was no closer, and I kicked off my shoes and dove in. I was a strong swimmer, so strong in fact I'd gone to BC on a swimming scholarship, and in just a few strokes I was yards closer.

"Alissa, hang on," I hollered with a mouth full of water.

"Bert?" she said, just loud enough for me to hear.

"Yeah, hang on," I said again. My arms burned as I stroked through the churning water. For just a second I thought of what it must have been like for Alissa to be in this water for hours. I swam faster. I reached her and wrapped my arms around her, kicking so we both stayed afloat.

"What are you doing?" Alissa said, pushing me away.

I spit out a mouthful of water. "The guys are getting the skiff and they'll be here in a few minutes. Are you hurt?" I asked, giving the parts I could see the once-over.

"No, but I think I'm caught on the net," she said.

I looked and sure enough she was. Somehow one of the buckles on her vest was tangled in the top of the net. "Can you kick your shoes off?" The last thing she needed was the extra weight of her shoes dragging her down. She nodded, and after a few seconds she told me they were off. "We've got to get rid of this vest too" I said. If for some reason the net shifted and, God forbid, went under, Alissa would too.

"Are you crazy!" she shrieked, panic clear in her eyes.

"Hey, hey," I said in a calming voice. "You're going to be okay. I'm here." I glanced over my shoulder and saw the skiff being lowered into the water. "Nothing's going to happen to you. Do you understand?"

Alissa looked at me for several precious moments before she nodded. An odd yet warm feeling passed through me at her faith in me, but I pushed it aside to decipher at another time.

"The skiff will be here in a minute." I tried to untangle her vest for several minutes but it was hopelessly snagged. I unbuckled it and eased her out of it.

"You know, there are other ways to get my attention," I said, trying to distract her from realizing the life vest was a lost cause. "You could have just called." I held in my sigh of relief when I saw the big net start to drift off.

"You didn't give me your number."

I smiled at her comment and the fact that she looked less frightened than when I first arrived. "Oh, yeah, right," I said, remembering my abrupt departure. "Sorry about that. Would you have called?"

"Probably not."

What? Probably not?

"I thought you were in some kind of trouble. I've had it with women in trouble with the law," she said, wiping water off her face.

"I think that's a story for another time," I said, hearing voices and the motor from the skiff approach. "Our ride's here," I said. "I wish it were a limo, but I'm a little off my game right now."

"It's perfect," Alissa said. "Thank you for rescuing me, again."

"My pleasure, m'lady," I said in a fake Knights of the Roundtable voice as the skiff pulled up beside us.

How I managed to joke about this was beyond me. My heart was still stuck somewhere in my throat, my pulse raced like I was sprinting, and my hands were shaking so bad I couldn't help Alissa climb into the skiff.

The shock of seeing her in the water had paralyzed me for an instant before reaction kicked in. I didn't remember thinking of what I needed to do. I just did it. One second my body was frozen in terror, and the next I was in the water swimming toward her. When I got close enough to see the panic in her eyes my adrenaline had kicked into overdrive. A sense of relief I couldn't even begin to describe flooded over me as Alissa was pulled out of the water—again.

CHAPTER TWENTY-TWO

Bert

My hands were still shaking hours after Alissa and I were back aboard the *Dream*. It was dark now, and between the *Dream*'s engines shutting down, Alissa in the water, and the skiff coming after us, the tuna were long gone. Alissa had stayed on the bridge with me as we pulled in the nets and prepared the boat for another try tomorrow.

The guys were their normal boisterous selves that evening, and I don't think anybody but I noticed Alissa had been quiet during dinner. When the galley had been cleared of the dinner dishes, instead of staying for a few games of cards, she excused herself. I was worried about her and followed shortly thereafter. I found her, a blanket wrapped around her shoulders, on the aft deck, very near where she went over.

"I wonder how many more lives I have," she said as I approached. I'd been quiet, trying not to disturb her.

"You were prepared, and that makes all the difference," I said. My words sounded lame, but that was the best I could come up with. "Mind if I join you?" She shook her head and I stepped closer, stopping beside her.

"It's something, you know," Alissa said. "Twice now I've almost lost my life, and neither time did it flash before my eyes."

I wasn't sure if I was supposed to say anything or let her continue talking. I risked it and chose the former. "I think they just say that in the movies and books."

"When I was in the water the first time I made myself think of things, remember events, people, that sort of thing. Anything to keep me from dwelling on where I was and speculating as to what was going to happen to me."

"I think that's perfectly normal," I replied, using my armchair psychology.

"Today I wasn't afraid, but all I thought about was you."

That I had no idea how to respond to.

"I thought about the way your face lights up when you smile. The way the sun glistens on your skin when you sweat. The way your muscles move and your body flows. The way the air rings when you laugh. How my body reacts when you're near. How it comes alive when you hold me. How incredibly sexy and desirable you are."

In any other instance I would know how to respond to *that*. I would step closer and take her in my arms. I'd tell her, *I almost died when I saw you in the water. I wanted, no, needed to rescue you and hold you and have you be safe. I'd tell you that you make me feel things that scare me and thrill me. I want to know every dip, hollow, and curve of your body. I want to feel your lips on mine, your tongue in my mouth, your hands on me. I want to look into your eyes and watch you come and hear you call out my name in the dark.* But this was no ordinary situation and I couldn't take advantage of it, so I simply said nothing.

"You're awfully quiet," Alissa said, pulling the blanket tighter over her shoulders. "I hope I haven't said the wrong thing and you want me to leave."

That confession shook me out of my stupor and I stepped closer, our shoulders touching. "I don't want you to leave," I said simply.

"What do you want?" she asked, anything but simply. When I didn't answer right away she added, "My grandfather always said go big or go home."

"He sounds like a smart man." I needed a few moments to gather my thoughts—and my nerve.

Alissa was still looking out over the stern into the calm water. "Go big," she said quietly.

"I want to kiss you," I said, giving her what she asked. "I want to run my hands over your body and feel your skin heat from my touch. I want to kiss the bend of your elbow, the crook of your neck, and that spot at the base of your spine. I want you to grab my hair and call my name when I put my mouth on you, my tongue inside you. I want you to be safe and warm and not afraid."

I waited for Alissa to respond, to say something—anything. As the seconds ticked by I grew more and more discouraged. Slowly Alissa turned and looked at me. Her eyes blazed in the moonlight, the look of desire erasing any sign of the fear and apprehension I saw earlier. She stepped closer, our breasts touching.

"I want that too."

❖

Bert

Holy shit, now what do I do? Well, I mean I know what to do, but what do I do? I couldn't kiss her, not here on deck. I didn't want my crew to see us. I didn't want to risk my integrity as the captain, and I didn't want them to get the wrong idea about Alissa. I mean Alissa and I were sharing a cabin, but we weren't…Jesus, what a stupid conversation going on in my head. This was private. What was going on between Alissa and me was very, very private.

"Your place or mine?" I managed to say and was rewarded with a smile that melted my insides.

"Yours. It's closer."

I liked the way that sounded, that Alissa couldn't wait to have her hands on me. "Good choice. I'm not sure I could have waited for weeks to get to yours." I stepped to the side. "After you." I extended my arm in a gallant gesture.

As Alissa passed by she said, "We'll see about that."

My pulse roared in my ears and my legs were suddenly weak. I followed Alissa across the deck and had to make a conscious effort not to stare at her ass or trip over my tongue. We were almost to the stairway when Rock's voice boomed over the deck speakers

"Captain to the bridge."

Fuck, just my luck. After months of celibacy I finally have a woman interested in me and am three minutes from having her naked in my bed, and duty calls. "Fuck." This time I said it out loud.

Alissa stopped and looked over her shoulder at me, her eyes dancing with promise. "I understand. Do what you need to do. You know where I'll be."

"What I want to do is you," I said, fighting my need to step closer. Rock could see us from his vantage point on the bridge.

"Hold that thought, Captain," Alissa said with a smile, then turned and went down the stairs.

It took a moment or three for me to pull myself together and make my feet take me up the stairs instead of down. "This had better be damned important," I said to the empty stairwell.

Fifteen minutes later my hand was shaking in anticipation as I reached for the doorknob to my cabin. I pulled away. Should I knock? Just go in? It was my cabin, for crying out loud. But I had a guest. Would I knock on my own bedroom door if I were at home?

WTF was I doing? Why was I overthinking this? Because I was nervous—more nervous than my first time. That made sense because that time it was hormones and three beers. This was... what?

When you're a kid it's lust, but as a woman it's desire. When you're a kid it's hormones, as a woman...what? The need to connect? A smooth exploration of another? A quenching of a thirst? Then why did I want to devour Alissa? To disappear inside her and watch her body respond to mine. Shit. I needed to get inside and I needed to do it now. I compromised and tapped twice, then opened the door.

The lights were on and I stopped breathing when I saw Alissa sitting in the desk chair fully clothed. I stepped inside and closed the door behind me. This wasn't what I expected to find. Had she changed her mind?

"Alissa?" She didn't answer right away. "Hey," I said, stepping closer. "It's okay if you've changed your mind," I said, lying smoothly.

Alissa stood and slowly closed the remaining distance between us. My heart thudded and my mouth was suddenly very dry.

"I didn't," she said huskily, her eyes wandering over my face and pausing on my lips. "Did you?" The way she was looking at my lips, the sound of her voice and her words made me forget how to talk, so I replied in the only way possible. I kissed her.

❖

Alissa

Bert's hands cupped my face and our eyes locked. If she didn't kiss me this instant, I was sure I'd go out of my fucking mind. I'd gone nuts waiting for her. I didn't know how long she'd be or even if she'd come. I refused to be in bed waiting ridiculously, because if she didn't show up I'd feel like a fool. Slowly she lowered her lips to mine. *Thank God.*

Her kiss was tentative, but I was way beyond tentative. Waiting for her had been agony, and I was more than ready to consider that foreplay. I grabbed her head, pulled her closer, and slipped my tongue in her mouth.

God, she tasted good. A combination of fresh air and woman. I deepened the kiss, wrapping my arms around her neck, and pressed my body against hers. She was soft and hard in all the right places, and my hands itched to verify which was which.

Still kissing her, I stepped back just far enough to get my hands between us and started to unbutton her shirt. I couldn't wait. Bert tried to help, but our hands got tangled up and I impatiently pushed hers away. She moved them to my ass instead.

I pulled her shirttail free from her pants and slid her shirt off her shoulders and down her arms. Grabbing her T-shirt I pulled it over her head, breaking her kiss for an instant before she pulled me back.

I let my hands wander over her bare back, the muscles hard and tight under my fingers. I moved them up her sides and around the front of her stomach. She sucked in when I lightly ran my nails over the flat, hard surface. We were both breathing fast, Bert's breasts moving against my shirt. I continued my exploration and cupped her breasts. They were the perfect size to fit in my hand, and when my fingers lightly grazed her nipples, Bert pulled her mouth from mine and moaned.

"Jesus, do that again."

I did as I was told, and with my mouth suddenly unoccupied I lowered my head and caught one nipple. Bert grabbed the back of my head and pulled my mouth closer.

"God, yes," I heard her say between breaths. She left one hand on the back of my head and, with the other, went to work on the buckle of my pants. In no time they were on the floor and her hand was on my bare ass. This time it was my turn to moan, or maybe it was both of us.

I reached for her pants, but Bert pulled my head up for another searing kiss. "We need to lie down on the bed or I'm going to take you right here like this." Her voice was raspy and breathless.

"No complaints from me," I managed to say as I snaked my hand into Bert's pants, past her boxers and into her. Her knees buckled.

"Whoa, Captain," I said, holding her up with a thigh between hers.

"I'm sorry," she breathed on me. "It's been so long, and it feels so good," she replied, grinding against me.

I pulled my fingers out of her, sliding them across her clit. She jumped and pushed against me harder.

"I need you naked," I said, tugging my shirt over my head. Thank God it was big enough that I didn't need to bother with the buttons, because I don't think I could have gotten them open. Bert crushed me to her, our mouths connecting again. I have no idea how we got the rest of our clothes off, but I do know the feel of Bert's body under me lit my fire even brighter.

Our arms and legs intertwined, we explored what we could reach. "I need to taste you," I said against her lips. Her answer was clear as she arched her back and lifted herself to me.

I quickly kissed my way down her torso. Next time, I told myself, I'd go slower and savor every sight, sound, and smoothness of her. This time, however, my crazy need for her drove me on.

"Open for me," I whispered, my mouth almost where I wanted it to be. The lights were on so I could see her perfectly. When she used both hands to do as I asked, my breathing stopped and I think time quit ticking as I looked at her. She was absolutely beautiful. Wet and ready for me. Bert Coughlin—captain extraordinaire, the most fascinating woman I'd ever met—was ready for me.

Slowly I bent my head and touched her with my tongue. She arched up into me, her hand slipping away and holding my head in that perfect place. She drew her knees up and let them fall to the side, giving me greater access to all that was her. With my tongue, I stroked her while I slipped a finger inside.

"God, yes," Bert gasped, which was all the encouragement I needed.

I slipped a second finger into her and looked up across her flat stomach. I wanted to see her, gaze into her eyes when she came. But what I saw instead took me over the edge, like slipping into the ocean that surrounded us.

Bert's head was thrown back, her back arched, her hips moving into me. Her hands were on her breasts, pinching her nipples. She was gasping with each flick of my tongue over her clit. I felt her stiffen and knew she was ready to come. I reached down, touching myself and mimicking what I was doing to Bert. I watched Bert as I imagined Bert's tongue on me instead of my own fingers.

Faster and faster I moved, the impending explosion developing deep in my belly and tasting Bert as she came. Both happened almost simultaneously, and stars shot through my head as Bert came in my mouth.

CHAPTER TWENTY-THREE

Bert

I felt my orgasm from the tip of my toes to the top of my head. It was by far the most powerful, intense climax of my life. It burned hot, and I couldn't have contained it if I tried. I couldn't think of a reason why I'd want to. As a matter of fact I couldn't even think. My mind was mush, my limbs felt like wet noodles. I think I might have hyperventilated because I was more than a little dizzy. My heart was pounding, but when I looked down to see if it was beating out of my chest, I saw Alissa looking up at me instead.

Her mouth was still on me, her fingers inside, but her eyes drilled into mine. Talk about an intimate moment. It didn't get more intimate than this. Nothing was more beautiful.

My clit twitched, and by the look in Alissa's eyes she felt it twitch too. I wanted more, wanted to feel her lips and tongue on me again, her hands on me, her body under me. Oddly I was suddenly shy, too shy to tell her what I wanted, so I showed her instead.

I slid my fingers in my mouth and slowly withdrew them. I repeated the action several more times, all the while watching the recognition burn in Alissa's eyes. Her eyes never left mine, and it didn't take long before our rhythms matched and I was on the brink again. I wanted to come with her, her tongue inside me, her finger dipping into my ass, but I wanted to taste her more.

Forcing myself back from the edge, I pulled Alissa toward me. "My turn," I said, moving her onto her back and sliding down. Her breasts were perfect, her nipples completely healed. I kissed each one. Alissa wrapped a leg around my thigh and pushed into me.

"Touch me." Her voice quivered with desire and I couldn't refuse. I'd never be able to refuse a request like this, or anything Alissa asked of me.

I gasped when my hand slid into warm wetness. "Oh my God. You feel so good," I said, my voice scratchy with desire.

I slid down quickly, so as not to be distracted from the other delicious parts of her body. I settled between her legs and kissed her lightly.

"Ugh." Alissa arched her back. "I can't go much longer."

"Do you want to?" I asked, wanting beyond anything to give her exactly what she wanted.

"No."

That was all the encouragement I needed.

I fucked her with my fingers, my nipples, my mouth. Alisa's body glowed with a fine layer of sweat, accompanied by gasps of pleasure and sighs of desire. Finally she grabbed my head, put my mouth where she wanted it, and spread her legs wider. With the beauty of it all, I found it hard to breathe.

❖

Alissa

When I woke, the lights were off, the covers pulled up, and I was nestled in Bert's arms. I felt her heartbeat kick up a notch or four, and the heat between my legs pressed against her hip. Quickly the events of the last few hours flooded through me and I couldn't help but panic. What had I done? I took a few deep breaths. Okay, I'd had sex, multiple times, but so what? Big deal. This couldn't go anywhere, but again, so what? As adults, we were certainly entitled to a little fun.

"Hey there," Bert said, her voice rumbling in my ear.

"Hey there yourself," I replied stupidly. We had exchanged bodily fluids, explored body orifices, and all I could come up with was 'Hey there'? For an advertising genius, I sounded pretty stupid.

"Are you okay?"

Was I okay? I'd just had the most mind-blowing, physically satisfying sex of my life, and I was trying not to freak. I was supposed to get up and go home, not want to do it again. "Yeah, you?"

"Mm-huh," Bert said flatly. Was it that bad? She didn't sound too enthusiastic.

We lay there silently in the dark. I could see the stars from the porthole, my view of the world around me. And what a perfect view. It was quiet—the only sound the low hum of the engines.

What was I supposed to say? This wasn't like any other hookup or casual, no-strings fling. I knew what to do in those situations, with those women. After Ariel, my relationships had been superficial and certainly didn't consist of pillow talk or morning-after, intimate chatter. I had no clue what to do about this. I found a safe topic.

"When we get back, I need to take you out on my boat."

"You don't have a boat, remember?"

"My new boat."

"Oh, that boat," Bert said. I sensed the smile on her face. "Have you thought about what you'll get?"

"I don't know. The one I had was a good size for me. It's just enough of a challenge to keep me interested and not too much to handle by myself."

"Do you take friends or a girlfriend out?"

"Yes, no," I said quickly.

Bert chuckled. "No to what? Friends or a girlfriend?"

"Yes to friends, no to girlfriends," I said, knowing this would open a can of worms I might not want to share.

"Did your girlfriends not sail? Get seasick?" Bert asked innocently. She was asking, not prying.

"My last girlfriend stole one million, four hundred eighty-two thousand, one hundred forty-nine dollars from my firm. That was four years ago. I've been a little gun-shy since."

"I can see why," Bert said, not hesitating. "Is she in jail?"

That was an interesting question. Most people didn't ask. I guess they thought embezzlement was a victimless crime and if it was paid back it was then okay.

"Prison. Four to ten years."

"Good. I'm sorry that happened to you."

"I appreciate that," I said, shifting to lie on top of her. I didn't want to talk about Ariel. Too many memories, too many questions, too many answers. I touched Bert's hair, remembering what it'd felt like when I ran my hands through it, when I grabbed to keep her close. It was soft and curly.

Bert adjusted the sheet to cover us both, her body warm beneath me. "Am I too heavy for you?"

"No, not at all," Bert replied. "You feel good."

I traced the outline of her jaw, her nose, eyes, and lips with my fingers. Her skin was soft, tanned by the sun. Laugh lines around her eyes were lighter than the rest of her face from her sunglasses, and her teeth were perfectly straight. She let me explore without interruption.

In a very short time Bert had affected me more than I expected. Sure, when we were having coffee I'd thought she was cute and someone I could have a fling with, but nothing more than that. I didn't do more than that. But these past weeks had shown me a side of her I never would have imagined and, to be quite honest, probably never would have hung around long enough to see. And here, in the night, in the afterglow, I wanted to know more.

The thought scared the ever-living crap out of me. I wasn't ready for this. I didn't want this. I couldn't risk this. I had to keep this light, and pillow talk was not included.

"How long do we have till we need to get up?"

Bert craned her neck to look at her clock, her body moving under me. My pulse beat a little faster.

"About three hours," she said.

I lowered my head to kiss her. "That'll be a good start," I said just before our lips met.

❖

Alissa

Slow down! Slow down! Unfortunately my body wasn't listening to my brain. The taste, the scent, the feel of Bert's body responding drove me crazy. I wanted to gobble her up like a piece of chewy candy, not savor her like an all-day sucker. My hands couldn't touch her everywhere fast enough. My mouth was even more impatient. My hunger for her was insatiable. I wanted her fast, hard, and right now. I drove into her time and time again, my need to possess overwhelming. Bert gripped my arm so tight I knew I'd sport a bruise in the morning. Her nails scraped my back so hard it stung, and her tongue was battling mine for control. She liked it this way. The more she gave the more I took, until finally she gave all and came hard. Bert stifled her screams in my neck as she trembled. She shuddered over and over, and on the third time I couldn't hold back any longer, and I followed her.

Wave after wave of bliss rolled through me. It was like a dam of molten lava exploding, mixed with sunshine. It felt so damn good. Nothing could describe it and absolutely nothing could compare.

We were drenched with sweat and gasping for air. I started to move off her, but Bert held me in place with one word.

"Stay."

She guided my head to her shoulder, pulled the covers up, and held me tight. Our hearts pounded, at times matching beats like our bodies were made to be together. I chuckled lightly.

"What?" Bert asked, smoothing my hair away from my face.

"It amazes me how something as simple as sex can feel so damn good."

"You think sex is simple?" Bert asked, her heart rate slowing.

"Sure. It's just a physical act. Touching the right place at the right time causes a reaction. If you're lucky, you have someone else doing the touching."

"Amen to that," Bert said, playfully slapping me on the butt.

"I bet you think I'm just a wham-bam kind of girl," I asked lightly.

"What do you mean?" Bert asked, clearly confused.

"It's been nothing but fast and furious for us."

"I'm not complaining." Bert pinched my butt.

"I can do slow and sensuous, you know."

"I'm sure you can."

"No, really, I can." I moved so I was now looking at Bert. Why was I saying this? It was like I needed her to know I was capable of more than how we'd just done it. What the hell? I never thought like this with other women. Why was I worried about this now? It's not like this was going anywhere. Since Ariel I never did slow and sensuous. That was too much like making love.

Bert pulled me up and cupped my face in her hands. "Alissa, what's this all about?"

What was this all about? Did I just say all that out loud? Not only had that last orgasm blown my mind, but I'd lost it as well. I needed to regroup, get my head back on straight. This was no different than what had happened with the other women I'd been with since Ariel, and I'd never told them much more than thanks.

"Alissa?" Bert asked again.

"I feel your heart beating."

"Don't change the subject."

"I'm not. I'm just making an observation." I silenced her rebuttal with a searing kiss.

I didn't want to think about this, and I certainly didn't want to answer any more questions. I had no idea why I opened that emotional door, and I slammed it shut before something scary could slip out.

Chapter Twenty-four

Bert

"God damn it." I was frustrated and tired, and my eyes hurt from scanning the waves and sonar all day. Nothing but a big fat empty sea. I knew they were out there somewhere. We had a huge school yesterday but lost them during the commotion of Alissa going overboard. What a mess that turned out to be.

Why did I think that? Alissa wasn't hurt and had ended up in my bed. Heat tore through me as images of last night flashed through my head. Alissa kissing my breasts, biting my nipples, looking up at me, her face between my legs, her back arched, grabbing my hair, holding me close, keeping me exactly where she needed me to be.

"Jesus," I said, shuffling and stomping my feet to get that image out of my mind. I needed to concentrate. I had work to do. Earlier I had Alissa go to the crow's nest with Hook. I had to get her out of my line of sight because every time I saw her smile or move an errant piece of her hair out of her face, it took me back to when she hovered over me.

"You all right, Captain?"

Crap. I'd forgotten Blow was on the bridge with me. "Yes, just frustrated we haven't seen any fish today," I said, the excuse convenient.

"Why don't you go downstairs and take a break. I've got this."

Maybe I did need a change of scenery or a cup of coffee. Or a stiff drink. Or another orgasm at the hands of Alissa Cooper. I couldn't focus. Jesus, I was really fucked.

Lefty was in the galley stirring a pot of something that smelled delicious. I was suddenly ravenous, realizing I hadn't had any lunch. I glanced at my watch. Ninety minutes till dinner.

"Can I get you something, Captain?"

"I need a quick snack, just something to hold me till dinner."

"Tough day today?" Lefty asked in his non-threatening way.

"Yep, nothing," I answered, taking a Sprite out of the fridge.

"Tomorrow is another day," he said, always the optimist. That and his cooking was why I enjoyed his company.

"How's Alissa doing?" he asked, his head in the freezer.

"Fine," I answered succinctly.

"She recover from her spill?"

"Yeah, she was a little shook up, but she's all right. I have her up in the nest with Hook."

"Can't get into much trouble up there."

"That's the whole point," I replied. I couldn't get into any trouble either if she was up there.

Lefty handed me three power bars and two cans of Coke. "Take these up to them. I'm sure they need a little something about now. Dinner's in an hour unless we're catching," he said, turning his back to me.

I whistled up to Hook and waved when he looked over the edge of the nest. I signaled him to drop the basket, and his head disappeared right before the line in front of me started moving. To save time and climbing up and down the ladder, I'd rigged up a basket attached to a rope and pulley. Whatever needed to go up to the nest could be placed in the basket and pulled up. Same for anything coming down. This also added an extra level of safety because nobody had to have anything in their hands while climbing.

I started to turn away when I heard someone coming down the stairs. I expected to see Alissa, but it was Hook.

"Need the head," he said.

"Take a break while you're at it." I tossed him the soda and snack. "I'll babysit," I said, winking at him.

"Yes ma'am," he replied, hurrying across the deck.

"Ahoy down there," Alissa called from thirty feet above my head.

I looked up and saw Alissa waving at me. "How're you doing?"

She put her hand to her ear, signaling she didn't hear me. I repeated my question. She still didn't hear it. The wind out here in the middle of the ocean was pretty strong and, up in the nest, even stronger. I put my boot on the first rung and started to climb.

It was tight quarters in the nest and even tighter with two. There was a stool to sit on, room for a small cooler with drink or snacks and not much else. Alissa had her back to me as I came up through the trap door in the floor. My eyes took the natural path up her legs, past her butt, and across her back. I stumbled when I pictured myself riding her bare ass last night.

"You okay?" Alissa asked when she turned around. She stepped back so I could close the hatch.

I had to lean over to close it, which put my ass in direct contact with her crotch. A jolt of something shot through me. Maybe this wasn't a good idea, I thought. "Yeah. How you doing up here?" I stepped as far away as I could in the suddenly very small space.

"Staying out of trouble." Alissa quirked her mouth.

"Mission accomplished," I replied, returning her smile. Alissa was relaxed so I decided I should be as well. I took a step and stood beside her, looking at the dying sunset.

"At least something went right today," I said flatly.

"You didn't have to rescue me."

I couldn't help but smile. "There is that, too."

It was comfortable standing here with Alissa. Our forearms were on the top of the railing, our skin touching. Everywhere I looked I saw water. Different shades, different patterns. It was calm now, but in an instant the ocean could turn into a powerful force of nature, destroying everything in its path. The wind caressed my hair and brushed over my cheek like a lover's touch. Good God. Where did that come from? Alissa's fingers traced a faded four-inch scar on my forearm. My skin heated under her touch.

"What happened here?"

"It's not a pretty story."

"I have a strong stomach."

"A jellyfish stung me a few years ago. My arm swelled and I bumped it on the door handle going into my cabin and it just kind of busted open."

"Ouch." Alissa traced it again.

"I'll spare you the gory details, but afterward it felt one hundred percent better."

"Did you see a doctor?"

"No."

"No? Bert, you could have died."

"We were in the middle of a trip," I said, as that was my excuse. "If it had gotten bad I would have called the coast guard."

"And you could have died before they got to you," she said adamantly.

"But I didn't. I was fine. I am fine—well, other than that." I nodded to the scar. "Lefty sewed it up, and I put butterfly bandages on it and wrapped it in gauze. It hurt like a S.O.B. for a few days, but I got through it."

Alissa turned to me an expression on her face I couldn't read. "Bert, I…"

Before she had a chance to finish her statement, the *Dream* hit a wave that knocked Alissa off her feet and into my arms. I instinctively put my hands around her waist, our bodies touching from breasts to knees. She gripped my arms.

We swayed together as the boat rocked in the swells. A spark I recognized flashed in Alissa's eyes, and my knees almost buckled. It had been almost ten hours since I'd touched her, and I immediately responded. My breathing became shallow and my mouth dry.

"Can they see us up here?" Alissa asked, her eyes on my lips.

"No."

"Good, because I really want to kiss you," she said, sliding her hands up my arms and into my hair. It didn't take much pulling on her part for me to close the gap between us.

Alissa's lips were soft and demanding, and soon the kiss was no longer a simple kiss. Alissa wrapped her arms around my neck and practically sucked me in. Our bodies were so close I could feel her erect nipples press against my chest. She surged against me when I slid a leg between hers. I moved one hand to her back, the other behind her thigh as she lifted it to press harder. I could feel the heat from between her legs and the wetness between mine. Almost frantically we rode each other until we came silently in each other's arms.

❖

Alissa

"Oh, my God," I breathed into Bert's neck. She tasted like sweat, passion, and sea air. "I didn't plan that." My hands were still shaking as I pulled them from around Bert's neck and slid them down her chest. Bert's heart was pounding. I couldn't meet her eyes. "I have no idea where that came from," I said, embarrassed.

I'd never done anything like that before. Never even been tempted, but for some reason I found myself at thirty-seven humping another woman in a crow's nest sixty feet from the ocean on a tuna boat. Wait until Rachel heard about this. Maybe I'd think about telling her. Or even though BFFs tell each other everything, maybe I'd just keep this to myself. I felt Bert's eyes on me as I tried to disengage myself from her arms and legs. Bert held me tight.

"Hey," she said softly

I still couldn't look at her. I was mortified. I was a grown woman. Never had I thrown myself at someone like I just had with Bert. I'd killed a whole bunch of *nevers* since I met her, and I didn't like it. Not at all.

"Alissa." Bert's voice sounded firmer. She put her finger under my chin and lifted it. I looked everywhere except her eyes.

"Alissa, look at me."

I lifted my eyes from my hands on Bert's arms, up her chest, past her neck and the pounding vein in her neck, past the lips I'd simply intended to just have a quick taste of, and into large green eyes.

"That was fucking awesome," she said, a grin spreading over her magic mouth. I started to relax. "I didn't come up here for that, but I sure am glad I did." The smile on her face was warm and inviting. "Okay?" She dipped her head a bit so she could look directly into my eyes. "Okay?" she repeated.

"Okay," I said, wanting to believe her. Why shouldn't I? I mean, she hadn't pushed me away. On the contrary, she'd pulled me in and come right after me. I guess she couldn't have hated it. She loosened her hold on me and let me step back.

We adjusted ourselves, and I found my hat that had fallen off during our romp, or whatever you'd call it. I squared it on my head and pulled my ponytail through the back. My clit was still throbbing. A whistle from the deck below drew Bert's attention from me. Thank God.

"Hook's back," she said. She waved at him and moved toward me. She took my face in her hands.

"For the record, you can jump me like that anytime."

Bert kissed me quickly, opened the hatch, and disappeared down the stairs.

❖

Dinner wasn't nearly as awkward as the remaining hour I spent in the nest with Hook. He'd innocently asked me about Bert's visit. I mumbled something and steered the conversation to a different topic.

Bert sat across from me and didn't say much. Thankfully the other guys kept the conversation going. I felt her eyes on me more than once, and my skin heated at the memory of that we'd done to each other.

"You okay, Alissa?" Hook asked, startling me.

I had no idea what he was talking about.

"You look a little flushed."

Oh my God. I forced myself to not look at Bert, the cause of my overheating. I hoped my voice sounded steadier than I felt.

"Yeah, I'm fine. I just bit into one of Lefty's jalapeno seeds in this salsa," I said, thinking of the first excuse that sounded even remotely plausible. Out of the corner of my eye I saw Bert shift in her chair.

I insisted on helping Lefty with the galley cleanup, even though it wasn't my turn. Blow didn't argue when I told him I'd take his shift. I was still rattled from what had happened earlier and needed some mind-numbing physical activity. Anything to stop thinking and distance myself from her physically and emotionally, especially emotionally.

I dried the plates and put them in the cupboard above my head. I was wiping off the table when Lefty said, "I think you've cleaned that spot three times."

"Oh, sorry," I said, obviously not paying attention to what I was doing.

"You okay?" Lefty asked. Out of all the guys he was the most observant. "You didn't say much at dinner."

"Who can get a word in edgewise with these guys," I asked. Lefty looked at me and frowned, knowing my excuse was bullshit.

I couldn't stall any longer so I left the galley. It was too soon to turn in so I went up on deck. Hook, Limpet, and Rock were sitting around a crew box playing cards.

"Alissa, come on. We need a fourth," Rock called, motioning me over.

I thought about begging off but couldn't come up with an excuse, so I sat down and they dealt me in.

When Bert approached a little while later, I was up sixteen matchsticks, two Coke-bottle lids, and three kitchen duties. The game was good for me because it forced me to concentrate and enjoy the company of these men and not dwell on what was going on in my head.

"I see you're playing for serious stakes," Bert said, pointing to the IOU chit for kitchen duties in front of me.

"Only the serious need apply, Captain," Limpet said. "I was winning until Rock invited Alissa to join us." All three men groaned when I dropped my hand, showing them my cards.

"Full house, gentlemen." I leaned forward and gathered my winnings—eight matchsticks, one more Coke lid, and an IOU for head cleaning.

"She's eating your lunch," Bert said from directly behind me. I could hear the smile in her voice.

Hook looked at his watch. "It's late, I'm turning in." Rock and Limpet agreed and followed him below deck. The thought crossed my mind that they were doing it to leave us alone.

"Looks like you caught on pretty quick," Bert said, moving and sitting in the seat Rock had just vacated. She sat back and crossed her legs, her hands in her lap. She smelled like soap and her hair was wet.

"I think they were just going easy on me."

"Trust me," Bert replied. "Those guys don't do anything, including playing cards, unless it's one hundred percent."

"Well, whatever the reason, I get out of three kitchen duties and one head cleaning." I waved the small pieces of paper in the air like a trophy.

"Are you avoiding me?" Bert asked quietly.

I started to say no but hesitated and answered honestly. "Maybe."

"Why?" When I didn't answer she asked, "Is it because of what happened in the nest?"

I looked at her even though my brain was telling me not to. A flashback of our little escapade earlier this afternoon clouded my brain.

"No." She held a hand up. "Let me rephrase that. Is it because we were alone together, and we jumped each other because we're hot for each other?"

"Maybe I just wanted to get out of kitchen duty," I said, tapping my pile of IOUs. Bert's smile made me start to relax.

"I'm the captain. I set the cleanup schedule."

"I wanted a free Coke?" I asked, holding up one of the caps I'd won.

"Meal and drinks are included in the passage."

"I needed some matches to light some candles?" I said, looking directly at her.

It was Bert's turn to hesitate. "Candles are not allowed on the *Dream*."

"Maybe I was trying not to follow you out of the galley and jump you again." I finally told her the real reason.

"Really?" Bert raised an eyebrow. God, she was cute when she did that.

I slowly crossed my heart with my finger. Bert watched, her eyes flickering as she licked her lips. "Cross my heart." My voice was a little breathless.

"Would you like to go to my cabin and talk about this a little more?"

"No."

Bert's eyes shot to mine, and she was obviously surprised. I stood up.

"I want to go to your cabin and let our bodies do the talking," I said just before turning and walking in that direction. The chair scraped behind me as Bert hurried to catch up.

There's something just downright sexy when a woman is confident enough to acknowledge she wants to have sex. I was no wallflower in that department, and Bert's reaction was more than a little thrilling. The fact that she desired me was a potent aphrodisiac. I wanted her hands on me almost as much as I needed mine on hers.

I felt her breath on my neck as we hurried down the hall to her cabin. The mere idea that we were intentionally going to have sex aroused me to the point of almost feeling in pain. There was nothing shy or surreptitious about what was about to happen. No accidental or subtle coupling. This was clear, premeditated intent. For someone who didn't want to be stuck on this ship for weeks, I couldn't get through the door and lock it fast enough.

CHAPTER TWENTY-FIVE

Bert

I had barely closed and locked the door when Alissa pushed me against it and started peeling off my clothes. I helped, and then we both took care of hers and had an almost exact repeat of what had happened in the crow's nest, but this time it was skin on skin. God, did it feel good.

I managed to get my hand between my leg and Alissa's center. She was hot and wet, and she whimpered when she rubbed her clit over the pad of one of my fingers. She was biting my neck and breasts, and within minutes she grabbed my head in both hands and kissed me hard. Our kiss muffled her moan as she came in my hand.

I lifted her and carried her to my bed. I knelt between her legs, and her knees fell open in a silent surrender as I dropped my mouth to her. I felt her pulse against my tongue and slipped two fingers into her as my tongue licked and flicked. Then I moved another finger just to the tip of her ass and pressed lightly, asking for permission to enter.

"Yes, please," Alissa whispered, her hand over her mouth so everyone in the entire boat couldn't hear her.

Slowly I entered her, and she started bucking harder. The image of her pinching her nipples, her juices on my face, my tongue on her clit was exquisite. When she came I felt it everywhere. She spasmed around my fingers, her clit twitched, and warm wetness coated everything. I was so aroused from watching her, giving this to her, all it took for me to come was for her to call out my name.

I heard my name softly penetrate the darkness and opened my eyes. My cheek was against the inside of her thigh, my fingers where I'd last put them. My limbs felt like jelly.

"Bert?" she called again.

"Hm-mm?" I replied, not wanting to leave where I was.

"I want to taste you."

My clit jumped. "I'm up for that," I mumbled.

When I started to move she said, "No, stay where you are. Just come up here."

Okay, I know my sex-filled brain wasn't firing on all cylinders, but stay where you are, just come up here? What the hell did that mean? I thought about it for a second, and then my clit jumped again. I got it.

I wasn't a contortionist so I couldn't stay exactly where I was, but after a few quick maneuvers I managed to get pretty close.

My heart hammered and my blood shot through my veins in anticipation as I slowly lowered myself to Alissa. She grabbed my hips and pulled me the remaining few inches until we were one.

I'd never been crazy about this position because I always found it hard to pay attention to what I was supposed to be doing and not what was being done to me. It never really worked well, and I always felt that either the woman I was with or I got the short end of the stick. But when Alissa's tongue touched me, I changed my mind completely.

We fell into a natural rhythm, and when she did to me what I was doing to her, I didn't want to turn back. It was my turn to cry out first, smothering the sound in Alissa's hot pussy. An instant later I felt her clit stiffen. She came hard, and I do mean hard.

Somehow I managed to move before I collapsed on top of her. I got my bearings and lay down, pulling her close.

We were both breathing hard, Alissa's breath on my damp skin chilling me. I wanted to pull the sheet up but didn't want to hide her glorious body.

"If you hadn't been avoiding me we would have done that much earlier, maybe even a few times. As it is, I don't think my heart can take much more than that," I said.

Alissa crawled on top of me, straddling my hips, her eyes bright with fire. "Let's find out."

My hips jumped when she started caressing her breasts. She was looking into my eyes, but I had to watch what she was doing. She pushed them together, then apart, then together again, all the while pinching her nipples—hard. I reached out to put my hands where hers were, and she swatted them away.

"You can look but not touch."

"What?" I asked, my voice hoarse.

"You heard me." She leaned forward, her nipples a tongue flick away from my mouth. I instinctively lifted my hands, but she backed away. "Don't touch," she said, teasing me.

She put fingers from each hand in her mouth, then pulled them out. She rubbed the wet finger around and over her nipple, and I swallowed hard. I wasn't sure I was breathing either.

She repeated the action, this time running her fingers across her stomach and stopping just before her pussy met mine. I watched in fascination as she opened her pussy lips to press closer to me.

I could see her clit glistening against me, and my head started to spin. I'd seen countless sunrises, watched the sun set over the ocean after a storm, but I'd never seen anything as exquisite as Alissa pleasuring herself. "I have to touch you," I stated weakly.

"No" was her equally weak reply. Holding herself open with one hand she rolled against me.

Holy Mary Mother of God, she was beautiful. Her hair was down, her skin glowed from the sun, and the expression of ecstasy on her face was almost too much for me.

I wanted to touch her. I had to touch her. I wanted my fingers where hers were, giving her unmentionable pleasure, my mouth on hers, breathing her air.

Alissa lifted her gaze from her fingers to look into my eyes. An instant later she came, and it was a long time before she fell into my arms.

"That was for banishing me to the crow's nest," she said.

It took me a minute to catch my breath. My head was trying to catch up to my racing heart. My ears were still ringing and I was light-headed. Watching Alissa pleasure herself was the sexiest, most sensual thing I had ever experienced.

I rolled her over onto her back. "Hmm, I'll have to send you up there again every day," I said before sliding down her body to feast on that warm, special place between her legs.

CHAPTER TWENTY-SIX

Alissa

Twelve days later we were within sight of land. The *Dream* had caught eighteen tons of tuna and safely transferred them to the transport nets. We trailed behind the transport boat, on standby if they ran into trouble. We played cards, told stories, and laughed a lot.

In the privacy of Bert's cabin we played strip poker, and when Bert realized I couldn't keep my hands off her when she started to lose, I'm sure she cheated more than once. But then again so did I.

We would dock in two days, and this exquisite adventure would be over. The guys were excited to get off the boat, but surprisingly I was ambivalent. What would happen with Bert and me? Would we continue this? And exactly what was *this*? Sex between us had become more hurried and more frequent as we got closer to shore. It was as if we both knew this would be over when we returned to port.

"We'll be docking around three tomorrow."

Bert's voice came over my right shoulder. I was standing at the bow of the *Dream* and felt her come up behind me before she spoke. These last few days I seemed to know where she was before I saw her.

"Okay," I replied. Actually it wasn't, but what was I going to say? *I want you to turn this boat around and just keep going. Let's sail away together?* Like that was going to happen. No way would this go anywhere. I didn't get involved, and obviously Bert didn't either. She'd said as much a few nights ago.

"How is it you don't have a girlfriend?" We were lying in bed catching our breath after another marathon sex explosion.

Bert laughed at my question. "This is an odd time and place to ask, isn't it?"

"Why do you say that?"

"I mean we just had mind-blowing sex—at least it was for me. I hope it was for you too."

"You know it was, you dummy." I poked her in the ribs. "Answer my question."

"I spent ten years building my business, and frankly, I didn't have the time or energy to put into it. That and the fact that this life isn't easy on the ones left behind. I saw what it did to my mom, and I won't do that to anybody." Her voice had lost its playful tone.

"But wasn't that her choice? I mean, didn't she marry your dad knowing he was a fisherman?"

"She did and she didn't. I mean she fell in love with him and because of that stayed with him, but she raised his kids alone and worried sick about him every time he went out. She didn't sleep hardly at all till he came home. Even then he wasn't around much. He was doing repairs to the boat, scouting new fishing grounds, hanging out with other captains and getting intel on where to catch. It's a hard life and even harder years ago."

"There was sonar back them, wasn't there?" I asked, trying to remember if I ever learned about the technology in high school. It sure as hell wasn't part of my undergrad or grad-school curriculum.

"Yes, but nothing like it is today," Bert answered. She didn't seem to think my question was dumb. "Sometimes it was hard to tell if it was a school of tuna, sharks, or a pod of whales. But for

some reason my mother loved him, had four kids, and spent most of her married life alone."

"Again, wasn't that her choice?"

Bert didn't speak for a while, then said, "I don't see your point."

"Couples do it all the time for whatever reason. Work locations, military spouses, hell, even prisoners. If both parties agree, then why not?"

"I won't do that to anyone."

"Why?"

"Because I believe in forever, and I don't think the trailing spouse has any idea what they're signing up for."

"Even if they come from a fishing family?"

"Especially if they do. Who would want to live like that?"

"Obviously a lot of people. Otherwise there wouldn't be so many little fishermen around," I said, trying to lighten the mood. What had started out as simple curiosity had become something serious.

"Maybe so, but not me."

"But just knowing you have someone, you belong to someone and they belong to you means something."

Bert didn't answer.

I'd intended the conversation to be over but couldn't help asking, "So you just hook up now and then?"

"No. I wait until I rescue a damsel in distress on the high seas and have my way with her."

I slid on top of her. Her hair was mussed from my hands in it, and she had sweat on her forehead. I wiped it off, my hand still shaking a bit. "Is that what you've done? Had your way with me?" I asked with false indignation.

"Yep."

"Is there anything we haven't done that you'd like to do?" I asked, curious at her answer.

Bert's eyes flashed, and I felt her heart beat a little faster under me. She smiled that smile that always got me going. Actually every smile got me going. It was working now.

"We've done things I've never imagined, so it's hard to say if we missed anything."

"Do you think sex is selfish?"

"What?" Bert asked, probably confused at my change of direction.

"Sex."

"I know what sex is."

"Yes, ma'am, you certainly do," I said, grinding my crotch against her hip. "Do you think it's selfish? I mean, when you have sex with someone it makes you feel good."

"I think all of my brain cells blew out the top of my head a few minutes ago so that's pretty obvious. But I don't think I'm following," Bert said, obviously confused.

I wasn't sure exactly what I was asking, but it was something I'd thought about often lately. "Okay, let me try to explain," I said. "You see someone you're attracted to, and your body gets all tingly."

"Tingly?" Bert asked. "Did you get all tingly when you saw me?"

"Yes, and then I got hot and horny, which is exactly my point. I wanted to have sex with you because of the way I felt. The way it made me feel."

"You wanted to have sex with me? Why the hell did we wait so long then?"

I poked Bert in the side. "Pay attention."

"Baby, you and sex will always have my attention." She squeezed my ass to demonstrate her point.

"I'm serious."

"I am too, can't you tell?" she asked, pushing me onto my back and sliding her thigh between my legs.

"That's exactly what I'm saying. I want to have sex with you because of the way it makes me feel."

"Okay," she said, readily agreeing.

"But don't you see? I want you to touch me because it feels good. And when I touch you it feels good to me. So sex is totally selfish." Made sense to me.

"Is there a problem with that?" Bert asked, nibbling on my neck in that spot that made my toes curl.

"No." I answered weakly, not sure anymore what my main point was or why I'd even brought this up. Bert shifted lower, my breasts her next place to taste. I tried to focus because I had a point in there somewhere, but when Bert slid lower I completely lost my mind.

"Alissa?" Bert's voice drew me out of my wet dream.

"Sorry, went somewhere else there for a minute."

"Wherever it was, by the look on your face I'd like to go with you."

"You were," I said simply, still watching the churn of the water from the powerful propellers. The sun setting in the distance.

"That's a pleasant thought."

"Pleasant doesn't even begin to describe it," I said, hip-bumping her.

"Don't do that," Bert said, stifling a moan. "I have work to do."

"You've never gone to work all hot and bothered to the point that you couldn't think straight?"

"Not before we rescued your cute little ass. Have you?"

A very unwanted image of Ariel and me on my desk flashed in my brain. I shook my head to get it out.

"That bad?"

"Not at the time," I admitted. Ariel had been an exquisite, attentive lover.

"The million-dollar girlfriend?"

I could say no and I might not have to talk about Ariel, or I could say yes and still might not have to talk about her.

"I refer to it as the million-dollar fuck."

"Ouch," Bert replied. "But then again, I've never experienced anything like that, thank God."

"Yeah, well, the only person I wish that on is Ariel herself," I said. "You know, her name wasn't even Ariel? It's Cindy Howard. How imaginative is that?"

"Maybe she wanted something more out of life."

"Yeah, my money," I said with more than a little bad taste in my mouth.

"Did she ever apologize," Bert asked.

I'd never been asked that question, but then again only a handful of people knew about my situation.

"Ariel? No way. Till the day she was sentenced, and even at her last parole hearing, she claimed I gave her the money. We were in love, I gave her everything because I loved her, blah, blah, bullshit," I said in my fake Ariel voice.

"Did you?"

"Yes."

"Do you?"

"No. It stopped the minute after the two FBI agents walked into my office."

"Wanna tell me about it?"

For some reason I did, so I started at the beginning and ended with why I was on my boat after the parole hearing.

"Wow," Bert said. "Sucked to be you."

"You can say that again," I said, scrunching my face.

"I would, but I'd rather suck you again."

Even though my heart was racing and my breathing had picked up, I slowly turned my head to face her. "I won't argue with that," I said and walked toward the stairs, thrilled at the knowledge that Bert would follow me.

CHAPTER TWENTY-SEVEN

Bert

I had docked the *Dream* hundreds of times, but this time I was anxious and nervous. Anxious because Alissa would be going home today, nervous because I didn't know what we were going to say to each other before she did.

We hadn't slept at all last night. We'd practically run to my cabin after dinner, the sound of catcalls and good-natured hoots from my crew, the peanut gallery, following us. We'd stopped pretending that nothing was going on when they'd stopped pretending they didn't see what was going on.

Alissa shrieked as I tossed her on the bed and started pulling off her clothes. I swear it was less than five minutes before we were both falling down the mountain of ecstasy we'd climbed together.

We always did it fast the first time. It was like we had so much pent-up desire it just exploded when we touched. I tried to slow down, but Alissa wouldn't let me. After that first time we didn't rush, but it felt like there was never enough time.

We knew this would end. When the *Dream* docked and the crew disembarked, Alissa would go with them. I wasn't relationship material, and Alissa was too gun-shy from that cunt Ariel. Who would blame her?

I scanned the dock, and in addition to Hook and Rock's families, I saw a man and woman I'd never seen. They definitely didn't belong here, in their upscale clothes and accompanying dark Town Car. They had to be Marie and Mark from Alissa's agency. Alissa had told me they'd insisted on meeting the boat, and she'd told them not to. I hoped they listened better about work things because obviously they hadn't listened to her about this.

Alissa was holding the starboard-side tether rope, ready to toss it to the dockhand. Her hat was pulled down low on her head, her ponytail out the hole in the back blowing in the late-afternoon breeze. Her arms were a wonderful shade of tan, in direct contrast to the paleness of the rest of her body. My crotch throbbed at that vision.

She stood with her legs apart, swaying with the motion of the boat as we pulled closer. The entire image was perfect and she was simply stunning, or breathtaking, or whatever word ever invented to describe what I was seeing.

The man and woman were jumping up and down, waving their arms. Obviously they were trying to get Alissa's attention. Ever the loyal crewmember, she ignored them and focused on her task.

❖

Alissa

In a few hours I'd be off this boat, my feet firmly back in my life. Back in my own house, my own clothes, my own job, and my own bed. They all sounded wonderful, but I wasn't as excited as I expected to be.

I'd thought a lot about this as we moved closer to this day, this moment. When I should have been getting more excited as the miles shortened, I wasn't. I wasn't looking forward to the things that made up my life. Traffic, unreasonable client demands, and those that thought just because my name was on the letterhead they owned me. The idea of hose and heels didn't appeal to me in the slightest, even if they did make my legs look fabulous. Meetings, endless phone calls, and airport security lines loomed like a big black hole. I'd probably lose my tan in a week, and my allergies to soot and bad air would kick in. Dinner parties, schmoozing, and being constantly on the lookout for new clients now seemed like, at worst, prostitution, or an endless bad movie at best. I wasn't sure which.

What had gotten into me? That was my life. I loved my life and everything about it, including those two clowns jumping up and down and waving on the dock. They reminded me of a scene in a war movie where the sailors returned after months at sea. Good grief, I'd only been gone for a few weeks and had talked to both of those goofballs twice a week. Sometimes that was more than we spoke when we were in the same office.

Shaking off my thoughts, I tossed my line to the dockhand, who secured it to the cleat bolted to the dock. When all was secure I signaled as much to Bert on the bridge. The late-afternoon sun reflected off the glass, but I was too far away to see her even if it hadn't been almost blinding me. Two blasts from the ship's air horn signaled we were secure aft and stern. One more thing checked off the end-of-trip list, one less thing to do before I had to leave.

I waved at Maria and Mark to get them to stop acting like fools and because I finally admitted I was glad to see them. They were the constant in my life, and after the past weeks I needed it. Finally they settled down.

"Friends of yours?" Hook asked carefully. He probably thought one of them was my girlfriend and didn't want to step into something ugly. I told him otherwise. "They work for me. The redhead is my assistant, the guy my main client manager."

"They sure are glad to see you," he said, stating the obvious.

"Well, to them this has been a nightmare."

"And to you?"

"A once-in-a-lifetime experience," I answered, looking toward the bridge.

❖

Alissa

I couldn't stall any longer. Everyone had departed, but I knew Bert was still on board—captain last one off the ship and all that. I felt guilty hanging around, thus keeping her on board, but I couldn't seem to get out of this cabin.

Her cabin. Our cabin. I looked around with a different eye than I'd had the first time I saw it. But then again I was a very different person. I'd been waterlogged, exhausted, and disoriented. This room and all it symbolized, including its occupant, had saved my life. Weeks later I was warm, dry, and full of experiences I'd never imagined. And leaving a woman I'd never thought I'd meet and would never forget.

Bert was nothing like the women I was usually attracted to, and I knew I'd never find anyone like her again. But that was okay because I wasn't looking. I could get great sex just about anywhere—okay, maybe not anywhere, but I could get what I needed when I needed it. I wasn't looking or even slightly interested in anything other than good conversation and an enjoyable time in bed. There was never a short supply of either, but my first priority was always Alissa Cooper Advertising. It always had been, and as long as my name was on the front door, it always would be. These past weeks were just a pause in that life.

After a light knock on the door, Bert walked in. Her hair was longer than the first day I saw her, her skin darker, and her eyes more troubled.

"Hey," she said, her voice husky.

"Hey." As I mimicked her, I cursed myself for not leaving earlier, when other people were around and it wouldn't have been this awkward. Who was I kidding? It would have been awkward regardless of who was around. The only positive thing about this scenario was at least I would get to kiss her good-bye one last time.

We'd said our good-byes all night without speaking a word, and when she'd kissed me tenderly before leaving the cabin this morning, I knew that kiss would be the last. It was soft, sweet, and poignant.

"Got all your things?"

My laugh sounded strained in the small space. "All my things are yours," I pointed out.

"You can keep them," she said, her smile forced.

"I'll just keep these," I said, plucking at the shirt and shorts I was wearing. "Either that or I walk off this boat the same way I came on—stark naked."

I realized what I'd said when Bert's eyes flashed. She moved toward me as if she couldn't stop herself.

"You might not want that, but I wouldn't complain," she said. That phrase was our go-to phrase because we said it a lot. It was our way of keeping things light when a comment or situation or question threatened to become too serious.

"You're such a dog," I said, trying to be playful in an otherwise intense situation. An image of the two of us in one specific and very fulfilling sexual position flashed through my head. It was suddenly very hot in the cabin.

"Well, I'd better go so you can get home." I gave her my best mock salute. "Permission to go ashore, Captain?"

Bert studied me for what felt like a lifetime. Her gaze never left my face, alternating between my eyes and my lips. I thought she was going to kiss me. I hoped she was going to kiss me. I prayed she'd kiss me. Instead, she stepped to the side so I could pass.

CHAPTER TWENTY-EIGHT

Bert

"God damn it to hell, motherfucker! Shit, that hurts!"

"It's true, sailors are quite imaginative with swear words."

My head hit the dash when Alissa's voice startled me. The stars that flashed in my head had to be from the knuckle I'd just smashed against the pipe or the concussion I just gave myself. It certainly couldn't be because Alissa was standing beside me for the first time in two months.

I slid out of the tight space I'd been working in and sat up. I stared at her perfectly polished toes, then gazed up her long, tan legs to short shorts and a tight T-shirt, past long strong arms, nibbleable neck, over lush, wet lips, and finally into bright, yet uncertain, eyes.

"Hey," I said, our standard greeting.

"Hey yourself," came the expected reply. "Am I interrupting?"

God. Her voice sounded better than I remembered and certainly better than it did in my dreams.

"Yes, but nothing that can't wait," I said, getting to my feet. I was a little dizzy, but that was probably due to getting up too fast.

"Permission to come aboard," Alissa asked, seeming nervous.

I didn't hesitate. "Absolutely." I didn't think the time was right to remind her that I'd never granted her permission to go ashore that day weeks ago. When she'd asked I hadn't said yes, but I hadn't said no either. Stepping aside like I had was the hardest thing I've ever done. I left it for Alissa to decide. And she had, loud and clear.

"What are you working on?" Alissa asked, looking at my tools and assorted nuts and bolts on the floor.

"Trying to wire new speakers."

"How'd the overhaul go?"

"No surprises, thank God." I wiped my hands on a rag. Alissa took a few steps closer and rubbed her hand over the captain's chair. "Have a seat," I said, finally remembering my manners. That's about all I remembered since hearing her voice.

"How was the catch?"

"One of the best." I couldn't help but smile remembering how good it felt to endorse the largest check I'd ever received. No ATM deposit for me. I went to the bank and handed it to the teller. I wanted no doubt where that money was going.

"How is Alissa Cooper Advertising?" I asked, since it was obvious we were staying on safe topics.

"Didn't fall down while I was gone."

"Good to know. You were worried about that."

"What's so surprising…" She ran her fingers over the dials on the dash in front of her. "I didn't even think about it most of the time."

"Is that a good or a bad thing?"

"Well, considering AC didn't crash and burn, it showed me I can get away and not work twenty-four seven."

"Also good to know." I wanted to stop all this chitchat and ask her why she'd come.

She'd called a few days after we docked, our conversation stilted and awkward, just like this one. We'd connected twice after that with the same result. If I'd had any thought we could continue something, those conversations proved we had nothing in common.

Her back was to me, so I could look at her as much as I wanted. She was a little thinner than I remembered, her back a little straighter. God, I missed her.

She turned to look at me. "I got a new boat." Her eyes were sparkling with excitement.

"Wonderful. What did you get?"

"Same as I had, just a year newer."

"I'm glad it all worked out for you."

"It was a royal pain the ass, but I finally got it settled."

The long stretch of silence was clear that we still didn't have anything else to say. Before, we'd always talked about something. If it wasn't boat-related, it was politics, the war on terror, or the pros and cons of nuclear power. We agreed on most things, but when we didn't, we agreed to disagree after a sometimes lengthy, spirited debate.

I struggled for a topic to keep Alissa right where she was. I've always been a pretty good conversationalist, and an even better bull-shitter, but my mind was blank. We didn't catch up like people do after not seeing each other for a while. No reminiscing about the things we did together. No strolling down memory lane, taking a detour to the time you took me right here on the bridge, or when we somehow made each other come in my too-small shower, or the quickie in the engine room when Lefty went to get a larger wrench. We couldn't even seem to talk about the poker game that lasted all night until Hook had all of our chits. Or how we laughed so hard during a game of Pictionary I thought Rock might hyperventilate. We would never go down that road where we looked into each other's eyes as pleasure rocked us to our core. No, obviously not. I fought back a wave of disappointment that threatened to overwhelm me.

"I promised you a ride on my boat," Alissa said, and I watched in fascination as she pulled herself together.

"You did." It wasn't a promise but an invitation said in passing.

"You free Saturday?"

If I wasn't, I was now. "Yes."

"The weather should be good."

"Should be." God, was I the queen of stupid comments or what?

"Would you like to take her out with me?" Alissa asked formally.

"I'd love to," I said, equally stiff.

"Eight o'clock?"

"Perfect."

"I'm in pier twenty-one, slip fourteen."

"I'll be there." That was a complete no-brainer.

Alissa looked like she was just about to say something else but instead looked around the bridge. She finally said, "Okay, see you then."

"What do I bring?" I asked, due to my mother's manners lessons.

"Not a thing, just yourself. I have everything we need."

We said our polite good-byes, and I watched her walk off the bridge. My heart was pounding, my pulse racing, and my hands were still shaking when I finally went back to work.

❖

Alissa

I don't know what was more difficult, going to see Bert again or walking away from her—again. God, she looked good, better than good. She looked fabulous. Her eyes were just as green and piercing, especially when she looked at me.

I had debated endlessly with myself about seeing her again. One day I was certain I'd put her in that place I put previous lovers, the next I was driving to the pier only to turn around before I rounded the last corner. As much as I wanted to, I couldn't bring myself to make that last few hundred yards until today. These past two months had been a mix of joy, reflection, despair, and everything in between.

The first week back at work was filled with mail, messages, and meetings. Everyone wanted to know the story from beginning to end, and of course they all asked at different times. Clients who knew I'd been out subtly or blatantly asked where I was, which caused more conversation. I certainly wasn't going to tell anyone what happened between Bert and me so I made up some story and just wished they'd stop asking. Good God, it wasn't like I was shipwrecked for years like Tom Hanks in *Castaway*.

The adjustment of being back in my house was surprisingly difficult. For some reason it just felt odd to sit in my spacious living room, in my kitchen that was enormous compared to Lefty's. My house was so much larger than I'd been used to for the weeks I was on the *Dream* that I felt like I was swimming in it—no pun intended. Everything seem oversized, too big and too quiet.

I loved my house. I'd bought it, remodeled, and furnished it after Ariel. It had taken me years to get it the way I wanted it, and it was my retreat, my energy source, and my place. I expected to be glad to be home, have my things, my own clothes, sleep in my own bed, and take a thirty-minute shower if I wanted to. This was my home, but it didn't quite feel like it. I felt a little detached, like I was just a visitor in a familiar place. My water was too hot, my clothes too restrictive, and my bed too big and lonely.

Maria and Mark had arranged to have a Welcome Home party for me, which was the very last thing I wanted or needed. I was sad to have left a great group of people, and I was having a hard-enough time coming to grips with the fact that I probably would never see them again. I guess it was like mourning a loss.

My friends and employees were thrilled to see me and wanted to hear every detail. They, like Maria, preconceived Bert's crew as a bunch of belly-scratching, beer-drinking, fart-and-belch guys that were one step down from low class. After correcting that impression about a dozen times, I gave up. No way could I describe the crew in ten words or less. It took me weeks to learn about them, and then I'd only scratched the surface of who they were. I liked and respected every single one of them. And then there was Bert.

No way could I adequately describe Bert the way I saw her. No way could I, nor did I want to. My relationship with her was mine, and I wasn't going to share, not even with my BFF Rachel.

"Come on, Al," Rachel said one evening shortly after I returned. We were having wings and beer at a local dive we both loved. "What was she like? Was she a bitch? A butch? A dyke?"

"No, she wasn't anything like that." I adamantly defended Bert's reputation.

"Then tell me." She was persistent.

How would I describe Bert? Confident, strong, fair, smart, witty, handsome, charming, cute, sexy, beautiful, stunning? A woman who could take your breath away with one look and set you on fire with another? I probably could go on and on if I wanted to. Before I had a chance to say anything, Rachel jumped in.

"You fell for her," she said, suddenly very excited.

"I did not," I replied quickly but admittedly with very little conviction.

"You did too. I can see it all over your face."

"What you see is fresh air, sunshine, and hard work."

"And lust."

"You can't be serious?" Rachel knew about my Ariel fiasco and my determination to remain single. "Pull your head out from between your legs, Rach. I did not fall for Bert. I admit she is attractive in that rough-and-tumble way, but I do not and will not fall for anyone. You know that as well as I do."

"Uh-huh," Rachel said, obviously not convinced.

"What does that mean?" I asked, somewhat testy.

"I mean your face lights up when you talk about her. Your voice goes up a notch, and you talk really fast."

"My face does that when I land a new client too," I said, effectively refuting her insane observation.

"Same kind of thing—see it, go after it, and capture it."

Okay, maybe not so effective, but Rachel was way off base and I told her so.

"We'll see," she said before reaching for the check. I hated it when she said that. And now here I was, two months later, going back out on the water with Bert, where it all began.

My flip-flops flipped and flopped on the pier as I walked back toward my car. I felt Bert watching me. The urge to turn around was almost overwhelming, but I forced myself to keep my eyes forward. What would it say if I turned around? Would it convey that I wanted to know if she was watching me? Was I interested or just following through on a vague invitation I'd made to her? If so, then why was I so nervous? Why had my knees shook when I boarded the *Dream*? Why had my heart pounded and the butterflies in my stomach taken off in flight?

When I'd approached the bridge I'd heard music, so I knew it had to be Bert. She'd said she spent most of her free time on the *Dream*, and when the gangplank was down I knew it would be her.

Bert had been lying on her back under the console to the left of the captain's chair. The weather was warm, and she was wearing a pair of cargo shorts I remember seeing in her drawer and a pair of well-worn deck shoes. Her legs were sticking out of the cabinet, and I'd flashed on a memory of them wrapped around me. That erotic memory had been sidetracked when she started cussing.

The sound of her voice had been like an accelerant to my frayed nerves. My heart beat faster and my hands were clammy. And when she'd scooted out from her small workspace and her eyes traveled up my body to mine, I was a mess. It was as if her eyes had transmitted some sort of heat ray or something equally bizarre, because my skin burned wherever she looked. By the time she reached my eyes I was about to melt or explode, I wasn't sure. But Bert didn't need to know that, and I didn't want to think about it. I'd fought too hard to put those thoughts out of my mind and failed miserably.

Our conversation had been ridiculous: small talk, benign, awkward chitchat. I'd thought a lot about what I'd say to her, but as soon as I'd felt the slow rock of the *Dream* under my feet, my practiced words completely dissolved into nothing. When I'd touched the captain's chair and flashed to what happened one particular night in that chair, I wasn't sure I would have remembered my own name. Jesus, when I'd asked her to visit my boat, I'd made my invitation sound as exciting as standing in line at the Department of Motor Vehicles.

The chirp of the security system on my car reminded me of just how much I hated it. A man walking toward me turned around to find the source and smiled at me when he realized it was my car. We nodded in polite greeting as we passed. I opened the door and practically fell into the driver's seat. I grabbed the steering wheel and dropped my forehead to my hands.

"Well, that went well," I said to myself. "Bert could tell you were thrilled to see her again. That you didn't sleep at all last night because you were so nervous about today."

Did Bert really want to go out on my boat, or did she just agree because it was the polite thing to do? She probably still considered me an idiot with more money than sense when it came to piloting a watercraft. Who else would let their boat catch fire?

The insurance adjuster had been a complete ass. He simply couldn't grasp the fact that *Adventures* was somewhere at the bottom of the ocean. I'm sure he'd seen his share of insurance scams, especially by an owner who wanted to pay for a boat they didn't want or no longer could afford. After many, many conversations with him and signing a document that said if my boat was found I'd go to jail for insurance fraud, I'd finally gotten my check and my new boat.

I'd christened her the *Smoke Alarm*, for obvious reasons, and had her out only twice so far. Because she was just a newer model, she handled about the same, and I was sure I could handle her with Bert aboard. Now all I had to do was prove it to myself, and I wasn't so sure I could do that.

CHAPTER TWENTY-NINE

Alissa

The brisk knock on my office door startled me, and my lawyer Paul walked in without waiting for an invitation. He closed the door behind him and hurried to my desk.

"What is it, Paul?" I was concerned. I'd never seen him this rattled, and I was still recovering from seeing Bert two days ago.

"Ariel's been released."

The room started to spin and I felt like I was in a vortex. I saw flashes of light behind my eyes and wasn't sure I could breathe. "When?" I managed to choke out.

"Two weeks ago."

"And we're just now hearing about it?" My mind was racing. Where was she? What was she doing? Was she plotting her revenge? Was she poisoning my clients? The list went on. I felt sick to my stomach.

"When I called, the parole board explained it as a bureaucratic error."

"Bureaucratic fuck-up is more like it," I said, getting my feet back under me.

"She is to have absolutely no contact with you, any member of your staff, or any previous or current clients. If she violates any of those stipulations, she goes back to prison to serve out the remainder of her sentence."

I could care less about the terms of her parole. She was *out*. "Maria!" I yelled loud enough so she would hear me through the closed door. It didn't take long for her to stick her head in and for me to start rattling off instructions. "Paul will get you a picture of a woman who is not allowed into this building under any circumstances. Send the same photo to the guard at the front gate to my neighborhood and the guard at the pier where my boat is docked. I want everyone in the conference room in fifteen minutes, no exceptions." Maria nodded and hustled out the door, closing it behind her.

"Do you think she'll do something?" he asked seriously.

"I have no fucking clue," I replied. "If I didn't know she was stealing from me when we were together, no way in hell will I know what she's up to now." I stood to go to the conference room. "She's had four years to do nothing but sit and think. And she's not stupid."

❖

Bert

It was a long three days. A very long three days until it was time to go to Alissa's. I couldn't remember a time I was ever this nervous. I ironed my shorts and T-shirt twice, pulled out my new pair of deck shoes, and got a fresh haircut even though I didn't need one.

I locked the door behind me and told myself that this was nothing more than a boat ride with an old friend on a beautiful day. I tried not to think about the chance that we might pick up where we left off. Based on our stilted conversation the few times we'd talked since we returned, that was obviously not going to happen. Then why was I walking so fast? Why was my stomach in knots and my knees a little weak? Why was my mouth dry and my hands clammy? I was so jittery I decided to walk to pier twenty-one. It wasn't far, but I couldn't sit in my living room any longer. Step after anxious step brought me closer to the unknown with Alissa and further away from what I knew best.

I stopped at the gate that would lead me down the dock to her boat. The gate was unlocked, so I pushed it open and stepped through.

The pier was lined with boats of all sizes, though a few empty slips had signs that they were normally filled. Those folks must have gotten an early start this morning. Alissa was in slip fourteen, which, since the odd numbers were on my left, would be on my right. I passed slip eight and counted ahead to fourteen.

The first thing I saw was Alissa, and then I didn't see anything else. That showed just how far my interests had changed. Most of my life I'd been as focused on boats as teenage boys are on cars. I could tell you the manufacturer and class of every boat I saw. But as I walked down the dock I didn't see any of them. All I saw was Alissa.

Silhouetted by the morning sun, she looked like a vision from some futuristic, fantasy place. White shorts exposed tanned legs, and a royal-blue tank top showed off everything else. She'd pulled her hair through the back of her cap, and she looked, well, for lack of a better word, furious.

She was arguing with a woman standing on the deck of her boat. The other woman was dressed stylishly in white pants and a dark-gray tank top. Her shoes were completely impractical for walking on the floating pier, let alone on any boat.

I didn't want to interrupt but I stepped forward anyway. It didn't take long before I could hear every word they said.

"Get off my boat." Alissa had more than a little anger in her voice. I would know. I'd heard it before.

"Lissa, please," the woman said.

Lissa?

"Don't call me that," Alissa said through clenched teeth. "I have nothing to say to you, Ariel. Oh, wait, that's not right. I have nothing to say to you, Cindy." She said the woman's name with a sneer.

Something was going on between these two, and I had no idea what. Clearly Alissa didn't like this woman—what did she call her—Ariel? Cindy? What was that all about? But I did know it was about to get ugly. It was none of my business so I stayed put, ready to step in if needed.

"Alissa, please let me explain," the woman pleaded. "I loved you, I really did."

"Now why don't I believe that? Let me ask, do you say the same thing to your husband?"

Husband? WTF?

"It's not the same. Robert is—"

"There's no way in hell I want to hear about your husband. I don't want to hear anything you have to say. Now get off my boat."

"You never gave me a chance to explain," the woman said, her voice a little more whiny.

"That's because no explanation can erase the fact that you used me to take my money and my clients. Nothing can explain that away."

Now it was all clear. This was the woman who stole from Alissa, the one she labeled the million-dollar fuck. I thought she was still in prison. Hopefully she was an escapee, not out on parole. I'd be the first to dial 9-1-1.

"It started that way, and then I fell in love with you."

Alissa laughed, her tone mocking. "You are so full of shit, Ariel. You lied from day one and you're lying now. You're a deceitful, conniving, manipulative bitch."

"You don't need to get ugly, Alissa."

Oh my God. This woman actually had the nerve to sound offended.

Alissa took a step toward the woman. "You don't get to tell me anything. Now get off my boat."

"Alissa," the woman said, her voice softening. She took a step closer and started to raise her hand. She was probably going to try to caress her cheek, but she could just as easily hit Alissa with a right cross. The first I didn't want, and the idea of the second was abhorrent.

"The lady asked you to leave," I said, my voice firm and commanding. Both women turned to look at me. They had been so involved in their argument, they hadn't seen me approach.

"This is none of your business," the woman said, looking at me dismissively.

"Yes, it is my business." I was almost snarling. "She asked you to leave. Now I suggest you go or I'll help you."

"You wouldn't dare," the woman said, more than a little indignant.

"Try me." Oh, yes, please try me. Nothing would give me greater satisfaction that to toss this perfectly coiffed woman in the drink.

"Bert," Alissa said tentatively. "It's okay."

"Yes, Bert, it's okay." The woman parroted her in a stickily sweet tone.

I stepped onto Alissa's boat and stopped inches from the woman.

"Who are you?" She turned to Alissa after looking me up and down. "Is *this* who you replaced me with?" I could feel the distaste in her voice.

I answered before Alissa could. "Who I am is none of your business. Alissa told you to get off her boat. I told you to get off her boat. Now get off her boat." I didn't raise my voice, which I found was a much more effective way of threatening someone. It worked, because the woman took a step backward.

"This isn't over, Al—"

"Alissa already said she has nothing to say to you." I took another step toward her, and she backed up another few steps.

"This isn't over, Alissa," she repeated, stepping carefully out onto the dock. She turned, and I thought she might say more but thought better of it. She spun on her high heel, almost falling into the water. Then she stomped up the dock and through the gate.

I turned to see Alissa standing by the wheel.

"I am so sorry you were in the middle of that," Alissa said, sounding subdued and more than a little embarrassed.

"Don't apologize. I put myself there. I know you're probably going to bite my head off and say you had it under control and didn't need me jumping in and rescuing you."

"No and yes," Alissa replied quickly. "No, I'm not going to bite your head off, and yes, I did have it under control."

"I know you did," I admitted. "I just couldn't stand by when she didn't leave after you told her to."

"That was Ariel, the woman who embezzled from me." She laughed. "But I guess you figured that out."

"Yeah."

Alissa moved toward me. I soaked up the sight of her, knowing that after today I'd probably never see her again. I'd given up on any chance of being with her again, chalking up our time together as just a good time precipitated by circumstance. But when I'd seen her standing in the doorway to my wheelhouse last week, my heart had jumped.

It was pretty obvious she'd shown up on my boat only to follow through on her invitation. She'd invited me on her boat in a passing comment, and I'd never intended her to follow through. When she'd committed to today, I'd leapt at her invitation even though I'd had to juggle a few previous commitments.

God, I missed her. I hadn't thought I would, but that was definitely not the case. I missed her smile, her wit and intelligence, the way she held her own with my crew, and the way she played cards. I missed our late-night conversations and pre-dawn sex. I'd admitted to myself weeks ago that I missed her in my bed. An image of her waiting for me wearing nothing but a mischievous smile flashed through my mind. We stared at each other for a few moments, and I watched, enthralled, as her face transformed from passive and expressionless to animated, then to something else. Her eyes burned, but she blinked a few times as if trying to regain control.

"Hey," she said, her voice sounding like light rain on a cool April afternoon.

"Permission to come aboard." I couldn't have hidden my smile even if I'd wanted to.

She stepped forward and held out her hand. "Permission granted."

Even though I was already on board, I wasn't going to turn down an opportunity to touch her again. A burst of heat shot through my hand all the way down to my toes when we touched. I almost stumbled under the sheer rightness of it all. "Welcome aboard the *Smoke Alarm*," Alissa said. "Pretty appropriate, wouldn't you say?" she added, seeing my amused expression.

"Absolutely." I handed her a box I'd had professionally gift-wrapped. "A christening gift."

"You didn't need to do that." Alissa dropped my hand to take the box. Damn.

"I wanted to." I'd had only three days to search for the perfect gift, and somehow I'd found exactly what I was looking for. "Open it." I wanted to watch her face when she saw it.

"Okay." She gingerly started tearing the paper at one end, then the other, then down the middle. It reminded me of the countless times she'd unwrapped me.

She looked at the dark box, then at me. The lid was imprinted with the image of a sailboat very similar to hers. That had just been luck. She lifted the lid, turned back the white tissue paper, and gasped.

"Oh my God, Bert." Her eyes darted back and forth between me and the contents of the box. She ran her hand lightly across the cover of the journal. "It's beautiful."

"You said you lost yours when your boat went down." The cover of the leather-bound journal had a mirror print of the boat on the lid. I'd had it inscribed in bold gold letters:

Captain's Log
Alissa Cooper

"Oh my God," she said again, her eyes glued to the book as she opened it. The creak of the leather binding was rich and warm. She turned a few pages of the thick, lined paper, caressing each page, then closed it.

"Thank you," she said, her voice a little raspy. "This is the most wonderful gift I've ever received."

Before I could react, she kissed me lightly on the cheek.

"Let me give you the grand tour," she said, taking my hand. I realized this was the first time we'd held hands. Hers felt warm, soft, and right. I certainly wasn't going to let go if she wasn't.

I paid more attention to the lilt in Alissa's voice, the graceful way her body moved, and the curve of her neck than I did to her rattling off the details of her boat. But I was able to recognize that it was a stunning vessel and suited her perfectly.

"Ready to head out?" she asked when we walked back upstairs.

"Any time." It was my turn to take orders, and the thought of watching Alissa on her boat was exciting. She had the carriage of a natural sailor, her confidence evident as she readied everything.

She was radiant, her eyes sparkled and her skin glistened in the early morning sun. She obviously belonged on the water, and I chastised myself for all the times I thought otherwise. I had definitely underestimated her and equally her impact on me. I pushed away those thoughts. Today was just about being with Alissa.

"What do you need me to do?"

CHAPTER THIRTY

Bert

We'd been out about an hour, and Alissa's mastery of her boat was unmistakable. She moved smoothly and confidently, almost anticipating what correction was needed before it actually was. Once we got out of the marina she stowed her cap, freeing her hair to blow in the light breeze. That was the perfect way to describe the look of freedom on her face. Sunglasses covered her eyes, protecting them from the glare of the water but preventing me from seeing them.

I'd learned to read Alissa's moods in her eyes. When they were bright she was excited, a shade darker meant she was concentrating, and when they flared, well, that was my personal favorite—*very* personal. Three days ago I'd caught a glimpse of all three, today only the first two, but simply looking at her took my breath away.

I watched her and wondered what she was thinking. Was she remembering the weeks we spent together? Did she relive almost every meal, every conversation, argument, debate, and laugh? Did she think about every time we made love? Did she ever think about me?

I found that I was enjoying myself. I was happiest on the water. Always had been and always would be. But this time with Alissa was nothing like I'd ever experienced. It wasn't because we'd done something fabulous or extraordinary or something I'd never done before. As a matter of fact we hadn't done anything at all. I usually wasn't very good at doing nothing. I always needed something to do, and on my boat something always needed attention. But I hadn't done a single thing since stepping aboard, and surprisingly I was content. And if I wasn't mistaken, Alissa was feeling the same. We'd barely spoken. The sound of the hull sliding through the water and the wind whipping the sail was all the conversation we needed.

Alissa caught me looking at her more than once, and I didn't even try to hide the fact that I was. She simply returned my smile and returned her gaze to the wide expanse of the ocean in front of us.

We'd been out probably a little more than two hours when she said, "I thought we'd stop and have a little snack and enjoy the day." She looked at me for confirmation.

"Sounds perfect."

"I've got some fruit and cheese below. I'll just be a minute." She started toward the stairs that led to her small but very efficient galley. As much as I enjoyed watching her walk away, I jumped up to follow.

"I'll give you a hand."

"Okay." She smiled one of the smiles that turned my legs into rubber and my heartbeat into what must have been twice its normal cadence.

I watched her as she filled a plate with grapes, cheese, a few orange slices, and some crackers. She'd stuck her sunglasses on the top of her cap, and with her long bare arms and legs, she was cute and breathtaking at the same time. She reached into the refrigerator, pulled out a couple of bottles of water, and grabbed some napkins from the shelf. She turned around and stopped directly in front of me. The only thing separating us was the width of the plate.

Our eyes locked and there it was. The third look I hadn't yet seen today, the one I didn't think I would. And now that I had, I knew what it meant, but I wasn't sure what it meant this time.

I didn't move. More specifically, I didn't want to. I wasn't sure I was even breathing. I caught the scent of everything that was Alissa. She smelled like freshness and sea air. She smelled like a breath of life.

I don't think she was aware of what she was doing, but she licked her lips, and my hands started to move to take the plate from her and pull her into my arms. She stepped back.

She swallowed a few times. "Let's go out on the deck. It's beautiful out there."

I wanted to say it was beautiful in here, but all the signs she was sending told me she wouldn't be receptive. "Alissa—"

"No," she said abruptly. "Please." Her voice had softened. "Let's just go up."

I could change her mind. I knew I could, but she might hate me if I did. I stepped out of the way so she could pass.

We ate and made small talk not much more important or personal than we had when she was aboard the *Dream* a few days ago.

"A friend of mine wants to meet you," she said after finishing her water.

Oh, fuck, is she trying to set me up with someone else? Can't get much clearer than that.

"Really?" was the only thing I managed to get past the bile in my throat.

"Yes. She said she wanted to meet the woman who saved my life."

"I didn't save your life. My boat was just in the right place at the right time."

Alissa grew quiet and played with a string on her shorts. I think she wanted to say more. Hoping it was in my favor, I kept my mouth shut.

"Actually, she wants to meet the woman I can't stop talking about."

Now that surprised the hell out of me. My pulse jumped as high as my hopes. "You can't stop talking about me?"

"Apparently not. At least that's what Rachel says. She's my BFF."

"What do you say?" I asked because, God help me, I wanted to know.

For every second I waited for Alissa to answer, my hopes climbed another notch. If it was something benign like she's a good captain, or she has a great crew, or she knows how to circle a school, she'd spit it out without hesitation. If it was something personal, well, that might take some time to get up the nerve to say.

"That you were the most interesting woman I'd ever met."

Big deal.

"That you were the only woman who has held my attention and challenged me in a very long time."

Ditto big deal.

"That you taught me how to play poker, bait a hook, and deal with being stranded in the ocean."

Triple big deal. I guess three strikes and I'm out.

"That you made me angry and crazy."

Into the dugout for me. It's going to be a very, very long ride home.

Finally she looked at me. "And that I had never been happier in my life than I was during the time I spent with you."

What did she say?

"You make me smile inside and out. I talk about you all the time because I think about you all the time. I wonder what you're doing and who you're doing it with. And, being completely unreasonable, I hope it's no one. You make me want to trust again."

Holy shit.

"I know we never talked about what would happen with us after we returned. I guess I just thought we'd go our separate ways and this would only be a very pleasant memory. Especially since you made it very clear that you would not be your father when it came to a woman."

I was stunned. I had no idea she felt this way.

"And then there's Ariel. She just about goddamned killed me. She certainly killed my faith in women. I was never going to get involved with anyone other than superficially. I would never allow myself to trust another person with everything I have, everything I am."

"Alissa."

She put her hand up. "No, don't say anything, Bert. I know how you feel and I respect that. I'm not going to try to change your mind. But when I was with you, I saw what I was missing, how empty my life was without you. So I talk about you all the time. Endlessly, constantly, because that's all I can have. And this." She indicated her boat and what we were doing today.

"So," she said, squaring her shoulders and sitting up a little straighter. "If that's what I can have, I'll take it."

That wasn't at all what I was expecting. I was hoping for something like "can we be friends," and I would settle for acquaintances. I hadn't even hoped for what I'd just heard.

"Say something, Bert."

"I'm afraid you caught me off guard." Her expression started to fall so I quickly leaned over and kissed her.

Obviously I'd surprised her because it was several moments before she started kissing me back. Our kisses were soft and gentle, and after several minutes I pulled away. As much as I wanted my lips on hers, I wanted to look in her eyes. Get lost in her eyes. Come home in her eyes.

"I'm an idiot," I said, sure of myself for the first time since Alissa walked off my boat. "I'm an idiot for thinking I could ever be happy without you. It ripped my guts out when you went down the gangplank, but I thought I was doing the right thing. At least I'd always thought it was the right thing. But I hadn't met you. And when I did, it all changed. Unfortunately it took me a few weeks to admit that to myself, and then I was miserable." Her face started to light up as my words sunk in.

"I am so full of shit." I laughed. "I used to think you can't miss something you don't have," I said, mocking my own words. "What a crock of crap. I was missing you before I ever met you. I just didn't know it. Even when you were a bitch."

"Purely a defensive mechanism," Alissa said.

"I figured that out."

"Thank God you did."

We looked into each other's eyes for quite some time,

"What do we do now?" Alissa asked.

"I've got an idea," I said, kissing her again, this time releasing the desire and need that were bursting to get out.

I forced myself to slow down as I kissed my way down her throat. Familiar, exciting sounds filled the air when I exposed Alissa's breasts and sucked her nipples.

"You are no idiot. You're brilliant."

I felt the warmth of the sun on my back when she pulled my shirt off and the smoothness of her leg as she slipped it between mine. Her shorts were no challenge to discard, and it would be hours before I would think about the wrinkles that would be in mine as I tossed them to the deck. The rocking of the boat matched the rhythm of our bodies as we made love. Or was it the other way around?

I keep my kisses butterfly-light and fleeting. Alissa shifts under me, a clear sign she enjoys what I'm doing to her.

I kiss up and down the valley between her breasts, the bend in her elbow, the curve of her jaw. My mouth paints her body like a canvas; her flesh heats and quivers under me.

I don't rush. I can't touch her enough. I love how her body responds to my caress, how she gives herself to me completely. I blow teasing breaths across the most sensitive parts of her body, and she shivers.

"Touch me, please," Alissa says, her voice raspy. I glance up and she is looking at me, the hunger in her eyes enflaming my desire. My tongue snakes out, just brushing her clit. She gasps, her delicate flesh quivering.

Her body is flushed with desire, her sex pulsing under my tongue. This is what I want. I am too far gone with need, my desire insatiable. I want to touch Alissa like she has never been touched. I feel her clit swell and I want more. She is incredible, the pounding of her heart under my tongue. I slip two fingers into her, and she cries out the most beautiful sound in the world—my name.

The explosion that rips through me is life-changing.

"Oh my God," Alissa said hours later, still panting a little. My heart soared, knowing she felt something as equally powerful as I had. This is what it must be like to make love. And I'd thought sex felt great, but this was indescribable. Alissa filled me, every hole of loneliness I'd ever had. Somehow I knew she would calm every fear, erase every insecurity, and conquer every doubt I would ever have if I let her.

"Oh, yeah, you're no idiot," she said into my neck. "You know exactly what you're doing. But your ass is going to get sunburned." Her hands glided over the body part she'd just referred to.

"Then I suppose I should turn over." I pulled Alissa on top of me.

By the end of the day we were both a little pink.

❖

Bert

"I want to see you again." We were sitting on the bench seat at the stern, a towel under our bare butts. Alissa was leaning back against me, our skin flushed from hours in the sun.

"I do too," Alissa didn't hesitate to say. "But I'll admit my brain is under the influence of severe afterglow, so what exactly does that mean?"

"What do you want it to mean?" *Jeez, Bert, that was a coward's response.*

"That we talk every day. See each other a few times a week or more. Go out to dinner, fishing, hang out with friends, watch TV, do what other couples do."

I turned Alissa around. This I had to say while looking into her eyes. "I don't want to see anyone else. I don't want you to see anyone else. I want to see you more than a few times a week. I want to meet your friends and your family. I want to watch stupid old movies with you and wonderful classic films. I want you to kiss me good-bye when you go to work and come home to *me*. I want to be your girlfriend and tell everyone you're mine. I want to make love with you and have wild sex with you. I want you in my life for the next eighty years."

Alissa sat perfectly still, but the pulse beating in her neck was running a marathon. Her eyes searched mine, and I poured everything I had, everything I was, and everything I wanted to be into them.

Finally, she smiled. "No complaints from me."

THE END

About the Author

Julie Cannon divides her time by being a corporate suit, a partner, mom, sister, friend, and writer. Julie and Laura, her wife, have lived in at least a half a dozen states, traveled around the world, and have an unending supply of dedicated friends. And of course the most important people in their lives are their three kids.

With the release of *Capsized* in February, 2016, Julie will have fourteen books published by Bold Strokes Books. Her first novel, *Come and Get Me*, was a finalist for the Golden Crown Literary Society's Best Lesbian Romance and Debut Author Awards. In 2012, her ninth novel, *Rescue Me*, was a finalist as Best Lesbian Romance from the prestigious Lambda Literary Society, and *I Remember* won the Golden Crown Literary Society's Best Lesbian Romance in 2014. Julie has also published five short stories in Bold Strokes anthologies. www.JulieCannon.com

Books Available from Bold Strokes Books

A Reunion to Remember by TJ Thomas. Reunited after a decade, Jo Adams and Rhonda Black must navigate a significant age difference, family dynamics, and their own desires and fears to explore an opportunity for love. (978-1-62639-534-3)

Built to Last by Aurora Rey. When Professor Olivia Bennett hires contractor Joss Bauer to restore her dilapidated farmhouse, she learns her heart, as much as her house, is in need of a renovation. (978-1-62639-552-7)

Capsized by Julie Cannon.What happens when a woman turns your life completely upside down? (978-1-62639-479-7)

Girls With Guns by Ali Vali, Carsen Taite, and Michelle Grubb. Three stories by three talented crime writers—Carsen Taite, Ali Vali, and Michelle Grubb—each packing her own special brand of heat. (978-1-62639-585-5)

Heartscapes by MJ Williamz. Will Odette ever recover her memory or is Jesse condemned to remember their love alone? (978-1-62639-532-9)

Murder on the Rocks by Clara Nipper. Detective Jill Rogers lives with two things on her mind: sex and murder. While an ice storm cripples Tulsa, two things stand in Jill's way: her lover and the DA. (978-1-62639-600-5)

Necromantia by Sheri Lewis Wohl. When seeing dead people is more than a movie tagline. (978-1-62639-611-1)

Salvation by I. Beacham. Claire's long-term partner now hates her, for all the wrong reasons, and she sees no future until she meets Regan, who challenges her to face the truth and find love. (978-1-62639-548-0)

Trigger by Jessica Webb. Dr. Kate Morrison races to discover how to defuse human bombs while learning to trust her increasingly strong feelings for the lead investigator, Sergeant Andy Wyles. (978-1-62639-669-2)

24/7 by Yolanda Wallace. When the trip of a lifetime becomes a pitched battle between life and death, will anyone survive? (978-1-62639-6-197)

A Return to Arms by Sheree Greer. When a police shooting makes national headlines, activists Folami and Toya struggle to balance their relationship and political allegiances, a struggle intensified after a fiery young artist enters their lives. (978-1-62639-6-814)

After the Fire by Emily Smith. Paramedic Connor Haus is convinced her time for love has come and gone, but when firefighter Logan Curtis comes into town, she learns it may not be too late after all. (978-1-62639-6-524)

Dian's Ghost by Justine Saracen. The road to genocide is paved with good intentions. (978-1-62639-5-947)

Fortunate Sum by M. Ullrich. Financial advisor Catherine Carter lives a calculated life, but after a collision with spunky Imogene

Harris (her latest client) and unsolicited predictions, Catherine finds herself facing an unexpected variable: Love. (978-1-62639-5-305)

Soul to Keep by Rebekah Weatherspoon. What *won't* a vampire do for love... (978-1-62639-6-166)

When I Knew You by KE Payne. Eight letters, three friends, two lovers, one secret. Can the past ever be forgiven? (978-1-62639-5-626)

Wild Shores by Radclyffe. Can two women on opposite sides of an oil spill find a way to save both a wildlife sanctuary and their hearts? (978-1-62639-6-456)

Love on Tap by Karis Walsh. Beer and romance are brewing for Tace Lomond when archaeologist Berit Katsaros comes into her life. (987-1-162639-564-0)

Love on the Red Rocks by Lisa Moreau. An unexpected romance at a lesbian resort forces Malley to face her greatest fears where she must choose between playing it safe or taking a chance at true happiness. (987-1-162639-660-9)

Tracker and the Spy by D. Jackson Leigh. There are lessons for all when Captain Tanisha is assigned untried pyro Kyle and a lovesick dragon horse for a mission to track the leader of a dangerous cult. (987-1-162639-448-3)

Whirlwind Romance by Kris Bryant. Will chasing the girl break Tristan's heart or give her something she's never had before? (987-1-162639-581-7)

Whiskey Sunrise by Missouri Vaun. Culture and religion collide when Lovey Porter, daughter of a local Baptist minister, falls for the handsome thrill-seeking moonshine runner, Royal Duval. (987-1-162639-519-0)

Dyre: By Moon's Light by Rachel E. Bailey. A young werewolf, Des, guards the aging leader of all the Packs: the Dyre. Stable employment—nice work, if you can get it…at least until silver bullets start to fly. (978-1-62639-6-623)

Fragile Wings by Rebecca S. Buck. In Roaring Twenties London, can Evelyn Hopkins find love with Jos Singleton or will the scars of the Great War crush her dreams? (978-1-62639-5-466)

Live and Love Again by Jan Gayle. Jessica Whitney could be Sarah Jarret's second chance at love, but their differences and Sarah's grief continue to come between their budding relationship. (978-1-62639-5-176)

Starstruck by Lesley Davis. Actress Cassidy Hayes and writer Aiden Darrow find out the hard way not all life-threatening drama is confined to the TV screen or the pages of a manuscript. (978-1-62639-5-237)

Stealing Sunshine by Tina Michele. Under the Central Florida sun, two women struggle between fear and love as a dangerous plot of deception and revenge threatens to steal priceless art and lives. (978-1-62639-4-452)

The Fifth Gospel by Michelle Grubb. Hiding a Vatican secret is dangerous—sharing the secret suicidal—can Felicity survive a perilous book tour, and will her PR specialist, Anna, be there when it's all over? (978-1-62639-4-476)

Cold to the Touch by Cari Hunter. A drug addict's murder is the start of a dangerous investigation for Detective Sanne Jensen and Dr. Meg Fielding, as they try to stop a killer with no conscience. (978-1-62639-526-8)

Forsaken by Laydin Michaels. The hunt for a killer teaches one woman that she must overcome her fear in order to love, and another that success is meaningless without happiness. (978-1-62639-481-0)

Infiltration by Jackie D. When a CIA breach is imminent, a Marine instructor must stop the attack while protecting her heart from being disarmed by a recruit. (978-1-62639-521-3)

Midnight at the Orpheus by Alyssa Linn Palmer. Two women desperate to make their way in the world, a man hell-bent on revenge, and a cop risking his career: all in a day's work in Capone's Chicago. (978-1-62639-607-4)

Spirit of the Dance by Mardi Alexander. Major Sorla Reardon's return to her family farm to heal threatens Riley Johnson's safe life when small-town secrets are revealed, and love may not conquer all. (978-1-62639-583-1)

Sweet Hearts by Melissa Brayden, Rachel Spangler, and Karis Walsh. Do you ever wonder *Whatever happened to...*? Find out when you reconnect with your favorite characters from Melissa Brayden's *Heart Block*, Rachel Spangler's *LoveLife*, and Karis Walsh's *Worth the Risk*. (978-1-62639-475-9)

Totally Worth It by Maggie Cummings. Who knew there's an all-lesbian condo community in the NYC suburbs? Join twenty-something BFFs Meg and Lexi at Bay West as they navigate friendships, love, and everything in between. (978-1-62639-512-1)

Illicit Artifacts by Stevie Mikayne. Her foster mother's death cracked open a secret world Jil never wanted to see…and now she has to pick up the stolen pieces. (978-1-62639-472-8)

Pathfinder by Gun Brooke. Heading for their new homeworld, Exodus's chief engineer Adina Vantressa and nurse Briar Lindemay carry game-changing secrets that may well cause them to lose everything when disaster strikes. (978-1-62639-444-5)

Prescription for Love by Radclyffe. Dr. Flannery Rivers finds herself attracted to the new ER chief, city girl Abigail Remy, and the incendiary mix of city and country, fire and ice, tradition and change is combustible. (978-1-62639-570-1)

Ready or Not by Melissa Brayden. Uptight Mallory Spencer finds relinquishing control to bartender Hope Sanders too tall an order in fast-paced New York City. (978-1-62639-443-8)

Summer Passion by MJ Williamz. Women loving women is forbidden in 1946 Hollywood, yet Jean and Maggie strive to keep their love alive and away from prying eyes. (978-1-62639-540-4)

The Princess and the Prix by Nell Stark. "Ugly duckling" Princess Alix of Monaco was resigned to loneliness until she met racecar driver Thalia d'Angelis. (978-1-62639-474-2)

Winter's Harbor by Aurora Rey. Lia Brooks isn't looking for love in Provincetown, but when she discovers chocolate croissants and pastry chef Alex McKinnon, her winter retreat quickly starts heating up. (978-1-62639-498-8)

The Time Before Now by Missouri Vaun. Vivian flees a disastrous affair, embarking on an epic, transformative journey to escape her past, until destiny introduces her to Ida, who helps her rediscover trust, love, and hope. (978-1-62639-446-9)